ASHES BENEATH THE ROBES

KUMAR AMARDEEP

Clever Fox® PUBLISHING

Chennai • Bangalore

CLEVER FOX PUBLISHING
Chennai, India

Published by CLEVER FOX PUBLISHING 2025

ISBN: 978-93-6707-425-1

CONTENTS

ABOUT THE BOOK

On a freezing night in Delhi, a homeless boy gives up his only blanket to save an abandoned infant, unwittingly setting off a chain of events that entangle him in a high-profile murder. What follows is a gripping journey through betrayal, justice, transformation, and revenge. 'Ashes beneath the robes' is a raw, emotionally charged tale of a street boy's transformation as a spiritual guru and fight for dignity in a world stacked against him. Will the truth set him free—or bury him deeper than lies ever could?

CHAPTER 1

A NIGHT OF CHOICES

It was one of the coldest nights Delhi had seen in years. The wind cut through the narrow lanes like invisible blades, and the fog hung low, blurring streetlights into a hazy yellow glow. On the edge of a busy market street, now silent and lifeless after dusk, sixteen-year-old Raju lay curled up on a footpath.

He had no home, no family. Just a torn, faded blanket — the only gift his mother left him before she passed away years ago. He held onto it like a sacred memory, the fabric frayed but full of warmth in ways only he could understand.

Despite wrapping himself tightly, the cold pierced through him. Sleep was a struggle, but Raju had learned to struggle and cope. Life on the streets taught him that comfort was a luxury, and survival was the only prayer worth whispering.

Then, in the silence of the night, he heard something — a faint, helpless cry.

A baby.

At first, he turned away, trying to ignore it. Delhi's nights were full of strange sounds. But the cry didn't stop. It was soft but persistent, like a call meant for someone. For him.

Raju sat up, eyes searching the shadows. Guided by the sound, he walked a few steps and spotted a small bundle lying near a closed shop's shutter. His heart skipped a beat.

It was a newborn girl, wrapped in thin cloth, her body trembling from the bitter cold. No one was around. No mother, no guardian. Just her — abandoned, innocent, and fragile.

Raju hesitated only for a moment before he gently lifted her. Her skin was ice-cold. Without thinking twice, he wrapped his only blanket around her. That blanket had protected him for years. Tonight, it was serving a new purpose.

His hands shook, not just from the cold but from the weight of the moment. He knew he couldn't care for her. But he couldn't walk away either. Holding her close to his chest, he ran towards a nearby hospital — a government clinic he knew stayed open at night.

He laid the baby gently at the entrance, securely. Before leaving, he whispered a silent prayer.

"Please... someone see her. Save her.
She deserves a chance."

He waited from a distance until he saw a nurse step outside and spot the baby. Relief washed over him. She was safe now. That was enough.

But now the cold struck harder. His body ached, his limbs numb. The blanket was gone, and the wind showed no mercy.

Where could he go?

One place came to his mind — an old, abandoned house near the outskirts of the neighborhood. People said it was haunted. Stories of screams, shadows, and spirits circled the area like folklore passed down to scare children. Raju had visited it a few times during the day, daring himself like boys do.

But tonight was different.

Tonight, it wasn't about courage. It was about survival.

He walked with hesitant steps, his breath forming pale clouds in the air. The gate creaked as he pushed it open. The house stood like a silent giant, its broken windows and peeling walls whispering forgotten stories. He remembered a room at the back — a corner where the wind didn't reach and the floor was dry.

He made his way in, heart pounding, every step echoing louder in the silence.

Sometimes, fear must take a back seat to necessity. When the choice is between fear and freezing, even ghosts can become friends.

As he lay down in that forgotten room, wrapping his arms around himself, he thought of the baby girl.

Maybe, just maybe, saving her was the reason he had survived so many nights before.

✦✦✦

CHAPTER 2

A BAG OF POSSIBILITIES

Sleep didn't come easily to Raju that night. Even with the cold numbing his body and the exhaustion in his bones, his mind kept drifting — to the baby girl, to the hospital, and to the warmth that once came from the torn blanket now gone.

As dawn broke, the golden light of the sun seeped through the cracked walls of the abandoned house. It painted everything with a dull amber glow. Raju sat up slowly, rubbing his arms for warmth. Then, something caught his eye.

A bag — placed a few feet away, half-hidden behind a broken wooden bench.

Curious, he approached it. It didn't look old or discarded. It was clean, almost new. Slowly, he opened it.

Inside were neatly folded clothes — new ones — for both boys and girls. And tucked between them was a small packet of money.

He froze.

Who had left it there? Why? Was it meant for someone? Was it a trap?

But hunger, cold, and survival often silence doubts.

He carefully picked two sets of clothes — one for himself and one for Radha.

Radha.

Just the thought of her brought a smile to his face, the kind of smile that came from memories warmer than any blanket. She lived on the same street with her mother, selling fresh marigolds and jasmine flowers outside a nearby temple. He had known her since they were children. They had shared food, laughter, and dreams under the open sky.

But not everything between them was simple.

Radha's mother never liked him. There was some old bitterness between their mothers — a story that Raju had never fully understood. But Radha never let that wall come between them.

He clutched the clothes close and ran. With the speed only a heart full of excitement could produce, he sprinted through narrow alleys, past shuttered shops, until he reached the place where he worked — a small general store tucked between two tea stalls.

He arrived before time.

The shop was still locked. A few minutes later, the owner came, surprised to see him standing there.

"You're here already?" he asked, raising an eyebrow. "Everything okay? You look like you haven't slept."

"All good, bhaiya," Raju replied with a grin. "Just couldn't sleep, so I came early."

The day passed slowly. As usual, the shop closed for two hours in the afternoon. Raju didn't waste a second. He rushed to the temple where Radha sat with her flower basket, her hands busy but her eyes always alert.

"Radha!" he called, waving to her.

She looked up and smiled. That smile — it made everything else fade away.

"Come, let's go for lunch," he said, pulling her gently. The temple often served free meals for the poor — sponsored by kind souls whose names Raju never knew but silently thanked.

They sat under the peepal tree, eating warm khichdi and sweet halwa. As they ate, Raju leaned in.

"I have something for you," he whispered, his eyes twinkling.

He took out the dress — somewhat new, and unmistakably expensive.

Radha's eyes widened.

"For me?"

He nodded. "And I've got one too. Tomorrow morning, let's go watch a movie, and then we'll eat at a proper restaurant — not roadside snacks, real food."

She laughed, unsure. "What about Amma? What will I tell her?"

"Tell her you sold extra flowers in the morning. I'll give you some money. And I'll talk to the shop owner — maybe he'll give me half a day off. I'll work late tonight to make up for it."

For a moment, there was only silence between them. Not the awkward kind — but the quiet that happens when two people see a little bit of their dreams becoming real.

It would be the first time they'd ever step inside a cinema first time they'd sit in a restaurant and eat like everyone else.

For a day, they wouldn't be street kids. They'd just be two teenagers in love, chasing joy.

They parted with promises in their eyes.

But while happiness was quietly blooming on one side of the city, darkness was taking shape elsewhere.

That same abandoned house where Raju had spent the night… had become a crime scene.

A little boy, chasing a rubber ball near the haunted building, had entered to retrieve it. What he found froze him in place — the lifeless bodies of a young couple, hidden in a corner of the house.

He screamed. Neighbors gathered. Police were called.

News spread fast. So did fear.

The same house that was once a home for ghosts in local tales… now held a much more real horror.

✦✦✦

CHAPTER 3

A DAY OF DREAMS, A NIGHT OF TRUTH

The police investigation had begun. The bodies discovered in the abandoned house sent shockwaves through Delhi's corridors of law and power.

What appeared to be just another runaway couple had a much deeper and more dangerous backstory.

The girl — Rajni Singh — was no ordinary name. She was the daughter of Diwan Singh, a powerful industrialist from Bhopal with deep political connections. A man whose name was spoken with both respect and fear.

The boy — Sahil — was the son of a domestic help who worked in Diwan Singh's mansion for years. A servant's son who dared to dream beyond his station dared to fall in love with a girl far above his social standing.

Their love was quiet, but defiant.

When Mr. Diwan learned of it, rage replaced reason. For him, it wasn't love — it was betrayal. An insult to his family's "honor". So, Rajni and Sahil fled to Delhi, staying in places known only to a trusted few. They had filed an application with the court, seeking protection and their right to marry freely — a basic right denied by pride and prejudice.

Now, they were dead.

For the police, it smelled of honor killing. Everything pointed to it. But the law doesn't move on suspicion — it moves on proof. And proof was what they didn't yet have.

Meanwhile, news broke like wildfire.

"Honor Killing in the Capital City"
"Rajni & Sahil Murdered in Cold Blood"
"Power, Politics, and Death"

Television debates exploded, hashtags trended, and public outrage soared.

But far from this chaos, two young hearts in another part of the city remained blissfully unaware. Raju and Radha were living their own little dream.

The next morning, they met early at the metro station. Both wore shy smiles and excitement in their eyes. They had traveled to the other side of Delhi — somewhere no one would recognize them.

In a large shopping complex, they found a clean public bathroom and changed into the new clothes Raju had found. The fit wasn't perfect, but it was good enough. Radha twirled once, checking her reflection. Raju stood beside her, fixing his collar. In the mirror, they saw something they rarely saw — not street kids, not orphans — but two ordinary teenagers getting ready for a date.

For a brief moment, they belonged.

They held hands as they stepped into the metro, as if sealing a promise between them — a promise of happiness, no matter how fleeting.

They bought tickets for the first show of the day. The theater was nearly empty. On the screen, a romantic movie played — full of laughter, tears, songs, and stolen glances.

In the dark, Raju and Radha smiled, whispered, and giggled. The innocence of first love is untouched by the cynicism of the world. Their hearts beat a little faster, not because of the film, but because they were next to someone who made life feel a little more beautiful.

After the movie, they walked hand-in-hand to a nearby restaurant. The menu felt like a foreign language, but they pointed at random dishes and waited eagerly. The food was hot, spicy, and delicious.

They laughed. They talked about nothing. And that nothing meant everything.

After lunch, they strolled through the now-busy shopping complex, their hands brushing against each other, their eyes taking to a world they seldom got to touch. But time was moving, and reality was calling them back.

They changed back into their old clothes, folded the new ones carefully, and took the metro back toward the life they knew.

As they stepped out of the station and were about to say goodbye, a sudden tap on Raju's shoulder froze everything.

A tall police officer with a thick moustache and sharp eyes stood before him.

"Are you Raju?" he asked, his voice cold and stern.

Raju blinked. "Yes…"

"Come with me."

Radha stood stunned, her hand still in his hand.

"What…what happened, saab?" she asked softly.

The officer didn't answer.

Dreams are fragile. And sometimes, they end before you even know you were dreaming.

CHAPTER 4

TRUTH ON TRIAL

Pressure was mounting.

The shocking murder of Rajni Singh and Sahil had not just ignited national outrage — it had also become a ticking time bomb for the Delhi Police. The media circus, the protest marches, the political debates — everyone demanded swift justice. The police, caught in the spot-light, knew they had to act fast.

So, the very next day, the Police Commissioner stood before a packed press conference room, his expression firm, voice steady.

"We have cracked the case," he announced.

Cameras clicked. Pens scribbled. The nation held its breath.

He continued, "The prime accused is a minor, orphaned boy (name withheld), living on the footpath, who has confessed to the double murder during our investigation."

The revelation stunned many.

A street boy?

But the police had come prepared. They presented a carefully constructed narrative — airtight, on the surface.

CCTV footage showed Raju entering the vicinity of the abandoned house on the night of the murder. Another camera captured him leaving — holding the dresses.

Then came footage from a shopping mall — the next morning — where Raju and a girl, identified as Radha, were seen entering the bathroom and coming out in different clothes. Those very clothes, police claimed, matched the outfits few days back worn by Rajni and Sahil.

Eyewitnesses were brought in. The owner of the shop where Raju worked said he had arrived unusually early that morning and appeared nervous. Radha and her mother also gave statements — innocently, but in ways that supported the police version.

The commissioner concluded with chilling finality, "The motive was robbery. The victims were killed for their clothes and money. The boy has confessed. As he is a minor, we are presenting him before the Juvenile Justice Board today."

Flashbulbs lit up the room. Breaking news crawled across every screen.

"Street Boy Killed Rich Couple for Clothes and Money: Police"
"From Footpath to Prison — The Dark Side of a Street Child"
"Confession of a Killer Minor Shocks Delhi"

But outside the echo chamber of official narratives, not everyone was buying it.

Social organizations, child rights groups, and opposition leaders weren't convinced.

"How can a sixteen-year-old boy overpower and murder two adults inside a haunted house, and then go enjoy a movie the next morning?" asked one activist.
"Where is the forensic report? Where's the murder weapon?" asked another.

Protests broke out across Delhi — at Jantar Mantar, at university campuses, outside police stations. Placards were raised:
"Truth Over Power"
"Don't Frame the Poor to Save the Powerful"

Meanwhile, Mr. Diwan Singh, the father of the deceased Rajni, began his own media campaign — cold, calculated, and well-funded.

He appeared on news channels, dressed in spotless white, grief painted on his face.
"Yes, I was against my daughter's decision. But I am a father… I would never kill my own blood," he said, his voice cracking at just the right moment.

Behind the scenes, he worked the phones — calling ministers, old friends, and business allies. Quietly, envelopes exchanged hands with select journalists. Slowly, news reports began to shift:

"Father Crushed by Daughter's Loss, Says Truth Will Prevail"
"Police Act Swiftly, Rich and Poor Both Under Law"

But the internet was not so easily controlled.

Independent journalists began digging deeper. One report revealed how Diwan Singh's men had been searching for Rajni and Sahil for weeks. Another uncovered a deleted social media message sent by Rajni to a women's rights NGO — requesting urgent help just days before her death.

The pressure was becoming uncontainable.

And with national elections looming, the ruling government couldn't afford more headlines screaming injustice. The protests had spread to other states. Students, activists, and civil society groups joined the chorus.

In a late-night statement, the Home Ministry made it official:

"Given the seriousness and public interest in the case, the investigation is being handed over to the Premier Bureau of Investigation."

The crowd at Jantar Mantar erupted in cheers.

Back in the small juvenile holding room, Raju sat alone. The confession they made him sign haunted his eyes. He didn't know what "Section 302" meant. He didn't understand why everyone believed he could be a killer.

All he had done was survive. And dream.

But in a world ruled by power and perception, dreams were dangerous.

✦✦✦

CHAPTER 5

THE PRICE OF SILENCE

The mobile phone buzzed in the dead of night, cutting through the silence like a warning shot.

Chetan Singh picked it up, his voice as cold as the Delhi air outside.

"Why are you calling? You were told not to."

From the other side came a hushed but firm voice. "Sir, we did what was asked. It's been a week now. Executing two people — and that too so cleanly — isn't child's play. We kept our word."

Chetan's jaw tightened. He paced across the marble floor of the bungalow.

"Yes, we've seen the news. It's everywhere. But didn't I say not to call? The phones might be tapped. Uncle gave strict instructions — no loose ends. You'll get your payment. Just wait for things to cool down. Two days. That's it."

The voice on the other end didn't flinch. "It doesn't work that way. We took the risk. If anything leaks—"

"Don't call again," Chetan snapped. "Your family will get the money. That's all you need to know."

He cut the call and deleted the number.

Far from the luxury homes and political whispers, a different kind of man was preparing to enter the storm.

Shashank Dhar, a senior officer with a spotless record and only months away from retirement, had been assigned to lead the investigation now taken over by the Premier Bureau. Known for his calm demeanor and sharp intuition, he was not easily swayed by power or fear.

Within days, Shashank and his team got to work. Call records were pulled. Bank accounts scanned. Forensic reports revisited. Witnesses re-interviewed.

From Bhopal to Delhi, the path of Rajni and Sahil was retraced.

It turned out their original plan was to hide in Agra, at a college friend's house, before heading to Delhi. They had contacted a lawyer — Shubham Tyagi — who promised court protection and an urgent marriage registration.

But soon, another truth emerged: Shubham Tyagi was a fake. A ghost with no law degree, no verified address, no past.

It wasn't a coincidence.

That man, investigators believed, was planted to lure them into a false sense of safety. Meanwhile, behind the scenes, Diwan Singh had struck a deal with one of the region's most feared criminal syndicates — the Dilawar Gang, known for contract killings and extortion across Western Uttar Pradesh, Haryana, and Delhi.

This wasn't about justice. It was about pride. To Diwan Singh, his daughter had not eloped — she had defied him. And that was a wound no amount of money or logic could heal.

Soon, arrests began. One by one, foot soldiers of the gang were caught. But their tongues were sealed tight with either fear or money.

Then came the arrest of Dilip Diwan, Diwan's son, who was seen in Delhi around the time of the murders. But even he gave up nothing. Cool. Calculated. Untouched.

And finally, Shashank had enough cause to bring in Diwan Singh himself for questioning. Despite pressure from political corridors to "go slow," the arrest was made quietly at night.

The media roared. The protests flared again.

But cracks soon appeared.

Two crucial questions hung in the air like unanswered prayers:

1. Who was the mysterious fake lawyer?
2. And how did Rajni and Sahil end up in the abandoned house, without appearing on a single surveillance camera?

That's when the pressure began to mount.

Ministers started calling. Senior bureaucrats whispered suggestions. Elections were around the corner, and Diwan Singh — with his money, manpower, and influence — was too important to alienate.

Shashank, who had spent a lifetime chasing truth, was now being nudged toward conclusion over clarity.

So, a "plausible" theory was prepared.

According to the final investigative summary:

1. Diwan's men had paid Munna Jat, a senior Dilawar Gang member, to trace Rajni.
2. Rajni and Sahil were found in Delhi on the eve of their court hearing.
3. They were kidnapped using a backroad route — avoiding cameras — and taken to the abandoned house as a temporary hiding spot, with plans to transport them back to Bhopal.

Then came the twist:

1. In the middle of the night, the couple managed to untie themselves.
2. As they tried to escape, they encountered Raju, whom they mistook as part of the gang.
3. A scuffle broke out. Raju, in panic, used a broken glass bottle.
4. Both Rajni and Sahil died. Raju, confused and afraid, took the bag with clothes and money — and ran.

The official line was complete.

Neat. Convincing. Clean enough to close the file.

Mr. Diwan immediately hired one of India's top legal teams. In court, his lawyers spun a new image of him — a father desperate to protect his daughter, not harm her.

"There was no intention to kill. He simply wanted his daughter back," the lawyers argued. "There is no direct evidence of murder planning," they claimed.

The case, already softened under pressure, began to crumble in public memory.

Diwan and his son were granted bail.

And Raju, the boy who once gave up his blanket to save a child, was declared guilty by the Juvenile Justice

Board — not as a murderer, but as a misguided child who needed "rehabilitation."

He was sentenced to three years in juvenile custody, with instructions to the state to provide him with education and life skills.

Outside the court, a journalist whispered to another, "So the rich walk out, and the poor boy pays the price."

The other replied, "No, the poor always pay. This boy just happened to get noticed."

And somewhere, in a cold room with iron bars and peeling paint, Raju stared at the ceiling, unable to understand where he had gone wrong.

He only remembered holding Radha's hand, dreaming of a movie, and that feeling of happiness… before it was all stolen by silence, secrets, and a system he could never fight.

✦✦✦

CHAPTER 6

THE FIRE WITHIN

The iron gates closed behind him with a metallic thud that echoed deep in his soul.

Raju, just sixteen, stood inside the juvenile correctional facility — wrongly accused, emotionally wrecked, and completely alone.

The first few days were unbearable. The walls seemed to mock him. The whispers of other inmates reminded him of the world's judgment. But what hurt the most was Radha's silence.

He often asked himself the same question again and again:

"Why did she say I did it?
Why did she stay silent?"

The betrayal, real or perceived, burned more than the cold floors he now called home.

He would lie awake at night, staring at the ceiling, replaying every moment of that day. The movie, the laughter, the goodbye… and the heavy hand on his shoulder that ended it all.

But pain is a strange sculptor — it can carve weakness into strength, and sorrow into clarity.

As the months passed, Raju began to adapt. The sharp edges of his grief slowly began to dull. He stopped asking "why me?" and started asking "what now?"

It was around that time he met Shyam Guru.

Once a celebrated motivational speaker, Shyam had fallen from grace after a domestic violence case — a charge he accepted with a calm head, calling it a "failure of character" in a moment of rage.

But prison hadn't silenced him—in fact, his voice had only grown louder within those walls. While serving time, he was assigned to visit juvenile correction facilities to inspire and motivate.

Every week, Shyam held informal 'mind power' sessions with young inmates.

"Life is not what happens to you," he often said, "it's what you decide to become in response to it."

Raju started attending those sessions quietly at first, sitting in the corner. But something about Shyam's words stirred something inside him — a flicker of possibility.

He began to imitate Shyam's speaking style during his free time. Practiced how he stood, how he paused, how he emphasized words.

Once, Shyam caught him mimicking.

Instead of scolding, he smiled and said, "The world breaks everyone, Raju. But afterward, some are strong at the broken places."

From that day, Shyam began to take him under his wing — teaching him not just how to speak, but how to believe again.

The turning point came on International Yoga Day.

A renowned spiritual figure, Fauji Baba, was visiting the correctional home as a guest of honor.

Clad in simple saffron robes with a robust army background, his presence radiated strength and peace in equal measure.

He led the boys through simple yoga poses, teaching them the power of breath and balance.

Then he delivered a short but unforgettable speech.

"Don't let your past define you. Mistakes are not the end — they are just the middle. Every night ends, and when the sun rises, it shines brighter on those who survived the storm."

He looked directly at Raju, walked over, and placed a warm hand on his head.

"Keep smiling. You will see bright sunshine one day. You are not a mistake— You are a story still being written."

At that moment, he became a seed of transformation in Raju's life.

For the first time, he felt like he could still matter.

Three years passed.

He walked out of the juvenile facility with no family waiting, no friend to greet him — but with a new strength in his spine and hope, quietly sitting on his shoulders.

As per the Juvenile Board's recommendation, the state government provided him with a small financial settlement, and a well-known NGO helped him find work.

He was placed in a local bakery, where he began working as an assistant, putting into practice the cake-baking skills he had learned during his time inside.

His days became structured, his nights silent.

He had survived hell. Now, he was baking sweet things for a world that had once turned bitter.

But one question still haunted him.

Radha.

Where was she? Why did she disappear?

He tried everything — visiting old corners, talking to temple vendors, even checking old shelters.

All he learned was that Radha and her mother had left the city soon after his arrest. No one had seen them again.

Did she feel guilty?
Was she forced to stay silent?
Or had she simply moved on?

He didn't know. And perhaps he never would.

But now and then, especially in the early mornings, when the bakery was still quiet, he would stare out of the window and imagine her standing beside him again — selling flowers, laughing with the wind.

And somewhere deep within, a silent promise echoed:

"One day, I'll find you. And I'll tell you...
I never stopped believing in us."

✦✦✦

CHAPTER 7

A KNOCK AT ROOM 603

The posters were everywhere.

"Kavi Vyas – The Truth, The Tears, The Laughter"
A massive show. The city was buzzing.

Raju had stopped in front of one such poster in the morning, admiring the man with a mic, mid-punchline, face frozen in comedic euphoria.

"Someday… if I can save enough," he thought, "maybe I'll see someone like him live."

But dreams were expensive. And life rarely allowed discounts.

By late evening, Raju was dusting the shelves and wiping counters in the bakery. The day's last cake — a premium three-layer truffle masterpiece — was sitting in the box, ready for dispatch.

The owner peeked from the kitchen.

"Raju, can you do me a favor? Can you deliver this last order ? Delivery boy has left for the day.
Before Raju could protest, the owner added, "It's for Kavi Vyas—for his wife's birthday. He's a big fan of our cakes and always orders from us whenever he's in Delhi."

Kavi's name electrified something in Raju.
"Of course, sir!" he replied, grinning.

He zipped through the traffic, reached the plush hotel, and passed the security check with the cake box. The lift was ornate, with mirrored walls.

Raju adjusted his hair and shirt in the reflection, trying to look respectable.
Room 603. He reached. Heart pounding. He knocked.

A woman opened the door. Pale, fragile, and possibly in her early 30s. Beautiful, but with eyes hollowed by silence.

"Happy Birthday, ma'am." Raju said softly, holding out the cake.

She tried to respond, but her knees buckled and she collapsed.

"Ma'am?" Raju rushed, catching her mid-fall, dragging her carefully to a nearby sofa.

The room was chaotic. Wine bottles scattered, a man in half-naked stupor snoring on the bed —unmistakably Kavi Vyas.

A hunter's whip lay on the floor like a sleeping serpent. The air smelled of cologne, alcohol, and cruelty.

He found water and sprinkled it on her. Her eyelids fluttered.

"Are you okay? Should I call for help?" he asked.

She shook her head. And then, with trembling lips and tears bursting out, she hugged him tightly.

"I don't want to live. He beats me, says it's a part of his 'creative process'— like pain fuels his jokes. Before every show, he beats me to a core. He continued beating me, till he got tired and fell asleep."

"I can't go to the police… my parents depend on his money. We're poor. He saved us once, and now we're his slaves..."

Raju stood frozen. His stomach twisted. He wasn't prepared for this.

"Maybe you can talk to someone… or a lawyer… an NGO?"

She shook her head, "Nobody listens. He's *Kavi Vyas*. He's a brand. Not a monster."

Raju got up. He just wanted to leave.
"I'm sorry… I hope things get better," he whispered, moving toward the door.

Just as his hand touched the handle, he heard a sudden gasp behind.

He turned.

Kavi Vyas was awake — eyes red, teeth clenched, rope in hand — grabbing the woman by the throat.

"You told him, didn't you? You filthy little—"

"I'll teach you what silence means!"

The woman choked, hands clawing at the rope.

Raju lunged — instinct, not thought.

He pulled, pushed, and shoved Kavi hard.

It all happened in one second.

Kavi slipped — his temple hitting the sharp edge of the study table with a sickening crack.

Then silence.

He collapsed.

The woman crawled to his body, shaking him, calling his name. No response. No breath.

Raju backed away, eyes wide.

"Not again. Not again. I didn't mean... I just..."

He ran.

Out the door, down the lift, through the lobby, past the security, into the shadows of the city.

His mind raced faster than his legs.

"Will they believe me this time?
Will anyone? Will she tell the truth to anyone else?"

Once again, fate had caught him in its web.

✦✦✦

CHAPTER 8

THE RIDE

Raju didn't sleep.

He wandered all night, like a ghost swallowed by the sprawling city. The narrow alleys, silent footpaths, and shuttered temples seemed to whisper stories of his past — of things lost, and hopes that refused to die.

But louder than all was the one sound he couldn't shake:
The sickening thud of Kavi's skull hitting the corner of the table.
It played on loop in his head like a curse.

Every barking dog sounded like a police siren. Every passing jeep made his heart freeze. His legs were trembling, but he couldn't stop. He didn't know where he was headed. He just knew he couldn't go back — not to the bakery, not to the NGO shelter. He had no home. No plan. Only fear.

By dawn, he collapsed on a worn-out bench near a temple park. The early sun peered through the trees like an indifferent observer. His shirt clung to his back, damp from sweat and anxiety. Legs numb, eyes red, heart racing.

And yet, beneath it all, something stirred inside —
A whisper.
A defiant voice:
"Not again. Not like last time. This time… I won't go down like a coward."

The world outside had already started spinning.

"Comedy King Kavi Vyas Dies in Hotel Room Under Suspicious Circumstances."
"Wife Critical in ICU, Mentions Assault in Private to Doctor."
"Juvenile Ex-Convict Seen Fleeing the Scene — Is Raju Back to His Old Ways?"

News anchors raised their voices. Hashtags trended.
#JusticeForKavi
#StreetCriminalStrikesAgain

The bakery register had his name. CCTV from the hotel lobby showed him entering the lift. That was enough for the vultures to gather.

Raju sat with his head bowed, rubbing his hands nervously, numbness gripping his thoughts.

That's when he felt it — a tap on his shoulder.

His body went stiff.

This is it. The police.

He murmured, barely audible, "Sir… I didn't do anything… it was a mistake…"

A deep voice responded, not harsh but firm:

"Come with us. Now."

He turned.

Two unfamiliar men stood before him. They weren't in uniform — no khaki, no badges. One of them opened the rear door of a black SUV parked beside the bench.

Before Raju could resist or even ask questions, the other man grabbed his arm and gently but firmly nudged him inside.

The car door slammed shut. The engine roared, and the vehicle sped off.

Another car followed closely behind.

"Who are you? Where are you taking me? Are you a police officer?" Raju asked, panic rising in his throat.

No reply.

He looked at the two men — serious faces, sharp eyes, minimal talk.

"I didn't kill anyone—he was hurting her—I didn't mean to… I didn't mean to!" he burst out.

The man in the passenger seat finally turned to him. Calm voice.
"Relax. Don't speak now. You'll understand soon."

Raju looked out of the tinted window. The familiar streets were disappearing. He had no clue where they were taking him. But somehow, it didn't feel like a kidnapping.

It felt like something else.

His heart was still pounding, but somewhere in the chaos of his mind, a quiet question surfaced: Were they here to save him — or bury him?

✦✦✦

CHAPTER 9

THE TRANSFORMATION

The car turned off the main road and entered through a grand arched gate.

"Fauji Baba Dham" — the golden letters gleamed above the gate, and a massive poster of Fauji Baba adorned the wall beside it, showing him with folded hands, eyes closed in serene grace.

But the car didn't stop at the main entrance. Instead, it veered to a smaller path around the back, away from the eyes of visitors and devotees.

It halted near a private doorway. The back door opened.

"Out," one of the men said, not unkindly.

Raju stepped out, confused and anxious. Just as he turned, another car door opened, and a man in his thirties emerged. He was tall, with an unsettling calm on his face. He wore flowing white robes, simple yet dignified

— the kind often seen on spiritual figures. His voice was steady.

"I'm Aniket Guru," he said, offering a slight bow. "Come with me."

Raju, dazed and unsure, followed him into the complex.

They walked through quiet, incense-scented corridors, lined with lamps and devotional paintings. The deeper they went, the grander the rooms became. Finally, they reached a large chamber — its walls covered with gods and goddesses, the furniture carved in intricate detail, the air thick with stillness and reverence.

At the center sat Fauji Baba — upright on a high-backed chair, hands on knees, his eyes partially closed. The same spiritual leader who had once visited Raju's correction home. But now, in his own domain, his presence was overpowering.

Aniket bowed deeply and said, "Jai Gurudev."

Raju followed, lowering his head in respect, though his mind spun with questions.

Aniket excused himself quietly. Fauji Baba motioned to the chair across from him.

"Sit, son," he said gently.

Raju hesitated, but the calm in the old man's voice gave him the courage. He sat.

Silence hung for a moment. Then, the spiritual guru pushed a glass of water toward Raju.

"Drink. You've been through a storm."

Raju took a sip, hands shaking. Then, his words tumbled out in desperation.

"I didn't do anything. It was a mistake… I didn't kill him on purpose… I was only trying to help… Please don't hand me over to the police. I can't go back to jail again…"

His voice cracked.

"Why am I here?" he finally asked.

Fauji Baba listened without interrupting, his gaze steady. Then he spoke.

"Do you remember the night you left a newborn girl at the hospital?"

Raju's eyes widened.

Fauji Baba continued, "I was there. I saw you. I took her in. She lives here now, in this ashram. She's growing, safe, and loved."

Raju's lips parted. He couldn't speak.

"Later," Baba said, "I met you in jail. I saw something in you. Not guilt — but grief, confusion, Innocence. I knew this recent crime was not yours either. The moment I heard your name in the news, I sent Aniket to find you… before the police did."

Raju clenched his fists. His voice trembled.

"Why? Why does this keep happening to me?

I never saw my father. My mother died when I was 12. I was imprisoned for a murder I never committed… and now again. Always accused, always hunted… Why me?"

Baba's eyes softened.

"Because injustice, my child, is often the crucible of transformation. It burns you — but in that fire, something stronger is forged."

He paused, then asked, "Do you know why I am called Fauji Baba?"

Raju shook his head.

The spiritual leader leaned back and began — his voice taking on the weight of memory.

"Twenty years ago, I was an Army officer. Newly married. Posted in Manipur.

One day, we were sent to neutralize an insurgent group hiding in a remote house. They had taken two civilians as shields — a young couple.

My mission was clear: take out the insurgents, save the couple.

We almost succeeded. As my men were escorting the couple out, their faces still covered, I spotted an insurgent aiming to shoot. I fired.

In the exchange of bullets, the couple was caught in the crossfire and injured. When we lifted the cloth from their faces… it was my wife. And her lover.

She died later. So did he.

People said I killed them out of rage. The Army didn't believe me. I lost everything — uniform, identity, sanity.

I wandered for years like a ghost, until a group of sadhus took me in. Seeing my background, they named me Fauji Baba. Slowly, I rebuilt— not a life, but a purpose."

Raju sat frozen. The pain in Baba's story mirrored his own — abandonment, accusation, loss.

"You're asking, 'Why me?' I asked the same. But life doesn't answer those who only mourn. It answers those who rise from the ashes."

Raju's eyes welled up. His lips trembled.

"But how will I survive now? The police are hunting me again."

Fauji Baba smiled.

"You won't. Because Raju doesn't exist anymore.

From today, the world will know you as Rajendra Guru.

This ashram is your rebirth. Aniket will guide your transformation."

Just then, Aniket returned, as if summoned by fate.

He offered his hand to Raju. "Come. We begin."

Raju stood slowly. He looked at Baba one last time.

Fauji Baba nodded, his face glowing with assurance.

"Be still, child. The world broke you twice.

Now, let's rebuild you on your own terms."

✦✦✦

CHAPTER 10

THE BECOMING OF RAJENDRA GURU

Transformation doesn't begin with noise. It begins in silence.

For Raju, the journey of becoming Rajendra Guru started not with robes or titles, but with something far more difficult—solitude.

The first few days in the ashram were quiet, almost eerily so. There was no bakery bell, no honking cars, no city clamor. Only the rhythmic ringing of temple bells at sunrise and the soft echo of chants from distant corridors. The silence gnawed at his nerves at first. He wasn't used to it. But slowly, the silence began to speak.

It spoke through the rustle of peepal leaves in the morning wind. Through the temple bells that sang at dawn. Through the calmness of Aniket Guru, who had now become his guide, teacher, and, unknowingly, a pillar.

Aniket taught him the discipline of yoga, the art of breath, and the power of stillness.

"Your thoughts," Aniket once said as they meditated beside a lotus pond, "are not you. They are just guests. Let them pass."

Every morning before sunrise, Raju would sit cross-legged under the Bodhi tree near the southern wall of the ashram. He'd breathe deeply, letting go of the past, even if for a few minutes. He didn't know when, but something inside him had started shifting.

From his body, the pain began to ease. From his face, the tension began to fade. A thick mustache now rested over his lips, and a long beard—once messy, now well-kept—grew over his face, giving him the aura of an emerging sage. Villagers who came for blessings started referring to him as "Guruji," and though he hesitated at first, eventually, he stopped correcting them.

Three months passed. He no longer walked with uncertainty. He flowed—between prayers, chores, study, and service. The ashram had absorbed him, and in return, offered him peace.

But it was Koyal who truly brought light into the quiet corridors of his healing heart.

She was now about four years old, full of curiosity, her eyes wide and alive. Everyone in the ashram called her *Koyal* for her melodious voice that chimed like a morning songbird. It was this girl — this abandoned soul he had once wrapped in a torn blanket — who unknowingly became his anchor.

Every evening, after prayer and before dusk, she would run into the inner courtyard to feed the sparrows. Rajendra would sit nearby on the steps, just watching her. She'd often sing made-up songs in a mix of broken Hindi and ashram chants, creating strange yet beautiful verses that made the older monks chuckle.

One day, as she handed him a mango from her basket, she asked innocently, "Guruji, were you always here?"

He smiled. "No, little one. Once, I was very far from here. Very lost."

"Were you sad?" she asked.

He nodded.

"What made you happy again?"

He looked at her soft brown eyes and said gently, "A voice. Yours."

From that day onward, Koyal sat beside him during evening prayers. She even mimicked his yoga poses, trying to balance on one foot and toppling over with laughter. She brought color to his grey — not with words, but with presence.

As months turned into a year, Aniket Guru became more than a teacher. He became an elder brother Raju never had.

Where Rajendra struggled with understanding scriptures or managing temple routines, Aniket patiently explained. When doubts returned like old ghosts, Aniket's voice always cut through with calm reassurance.

In private, they often sat by the ashram fire after others had gone to sleep. There, they shared silences and sometimes memories. Aniket rarely spoke of his own past, but Rajendra didn't ask. Some wounds need no voice.

To the world, Rajendra was now "Guruji." He walked in white robes. He led morning meditations. He helped prepare food for the poor. He sat beside Fauji Baba during weekly sermons. The crowd had started noticing his presence, his stillness.

But even as he embraced this new life, deep inside, a part of Raju remained — the boy from the Delhi footpath who had known what it meant to be forgotten.

And maybe that was his strength.

The Assignment

It was a calm evening after the final *aarti*. The sky above the ashram glowed with a fading orange hue, and chants slowly died down as devotees dispersed.

Aniket approached Rajendra as he stood near the temple lamps.

"Come," he said quietly. "Fauji Baba has something we must discuss."

They walked together to the smaller meditation hall. Aniket closed the door and took out a folder from the nearby shelf.

From it, he pulled out a photograph and slid it across the wooden table.

"Do you know this man?" he asked.

Rajendra picked it up. His face stiffened.

"How can I forget him?" he muttered.

The picture was of Diwan Singh — a man of sharp features, stern eyes, and arrogance that bled through the still frame. Rajendra had seen him years ago, during court trials, when Diwan Singh's name was whispered in shady circles — a man with immense political clout and a spine made of ice.

Aniket nodded. “Well, Fauji Baba doesn’t like him either.”

He took a slow breath and continued. “Long back, Fauji Baba had tried to start a spiritual center in Bhopal. Everything was lined up. But Diwan Singh, using his influence, got the land allocation canceled. That land was later handed over to Shri Mahan Baba — a controversial figure in Bhopal, whom Diwan Singh openly supports.”

Rajendra was silent. The picture still rested in his hand.

Aniket’s voice became firm but hopeful.

“Now, a new opportunity has come. A chance to set up our own ashram there.
Fauji Baba wants *you* to go. To lead the mission.”

Rajendra blinked.

“Me? But... how will I manage something like that?”

Aniket smiled, placing a hand on his shoulder.

“Don’t worry about that. I will handle the logistics, contacts, and papers. You will carry the spirit. The people will feel your sincerity.”

There was a silence between them. Not heavy — but filled with unspoken faith.

Rajendra looked at the picture again.

This wasn't just a new project. This was a test — maybe even a calling.

A city where his Guru had once faced defeat. A land ruled by influence and control.
Could the boy once accused of crimes now build a place of peace and purpose?

"I'll go," he said finally, his voice quiet but resolute.

Aniket smiled.

"I never doubted that."

As the Night Settled

That night, Rajendra stood at the temple terrace under a moonlit sky. Koyal was asleep. Aniket was at his quarters. The air was still.

He looked down at the ashram — this sanctuary of second chances — and whispered to himself:

"Maybe life didn't punish me after all. Maybe… it was preparing me."

He was no longer running from his past.

He was walking toward his purpose.

And in the distance, the lights of Bhopal flickered like stars—waiting, watching, testing.

✦✦✦

CHAPTER 11

SHADOWS BEHIND THE GRANDEUR

The mansion of Mr. Diwan Singh glowed like a golden fortress under the arc-lights of celebration. From the towering gates embossed with lions to the marble fountains that shot water in choreographed rhythms, everything screamed wealth, power, and control.

Inside, decorators moved like bees—draping silks, polishing chandeliers, placing flowers flown in from Ooty, ironing curtains embroidered with real gold thread. Diwan Singh had left no stone unturned.

After all, this was no ordinary party.

Dilip Diwan, his only son, was returning home after four years of self-imposed exile. The world had forgotten the headlines, but those close to the family remembered too well: "Heir Accused in Sister's Tragic Death," "Family Scandal Rocks Business Empire."

Diwan Singh had shipped him off quietly to Europe, away from gossip, courts, and shame. And now, with time as his shield and reputation partially restored, the patriarch had decided to bring his son back into the fold—into the lion's den.

Dilip Diwan stepped out of the sleek black SUV wearing a simple white shirt and navy trousers. Clean-shaven, lean, with quiet eyes that held more pain than pride. Servants rushed to greet him, bowing low, but he hardly noticed. His eyes scanned the mansion not with nostalgia, but caution.

Inside the house, Chandraprabha Singh, his mother, was directing the floral arrangements in the central hallway with her hawk-like gaze.

"Bring the jasmine to the center arch, not left! And that curtain—crease it properly. You think this is a tea stall?" she barked at the decorators, who scurried like terrified mice.

She spotted Dilip and walked toward him with a stiff smile. "You're late," she said.

He nodded quietly, "The flight—"

"I told you to come a day early. No excuses in this house, especially not for you."

She didn't hug him. That wasn't her way. She simply turned and walked away, knowing he'd follow. And he did.

In the grand dining hall, Chetan, Diwan's nephew, was holding court. Dressed in a crisp cream kurta with a designer watch flashing under his sleeve, he was laughing with two of the local politicians who would be attending tonight.

Chetan had the same sharp jawline as his uncle, but with a youthfulness that allowed him to charm as easily as he intimidated. Many insiders already whispered—*Chetan is the real heir, bloodline be damned.*

He spotted Dilip and smirked. "Well, look who rose from the ashes."

Dilip gave a polite nod. "Good to see you, Chetan bhai."

Chetan put a friendly arm around his shoulder, but his grip was tight. "Let's see how long you last this time."

Diwan Singh entered at that moment. Everyone straightened.

He walked toward his son and studied him. No words, just a long pause.

Finally, he spoke.

"You'll start attending factory board meetings from next week. Time, you stop being a ghost."

Dilip didn't answer. But in his eyes, something flickered—was it resistance, or simply exhaustion?

At the backside of the mansion, a bus pulled in, honking sharply. Dust rose as tired eyes and calloused hands stepped down. Workers—sourced from Diwan's many textile factories—had been summoned to assist with the party prep.

Among them was a girl with a fire in her eyes and a stubborn stillness in her walk. Radha.

She hadn't wanted to come.

Her past with the Diwan family still burned in her memory like fresh wounds. They were the reason she lost her first love.

"Get ready fast, Radha," her mother had pleaded that morning. "We owe our roof to Mr. Diwan's mercy. Don't forget where your food comes from."

But Radha never forgot the other truth: where her pain had come from.

Now, dressed in a plain yellow salwar suit, she walked into the mansion through the servant entrance with a cloth tied around her head, holding a broom and a bucket.

Inside, they were quickly assigned tasks. Radha was told to clean the guest rooms on the west wing—luxury suites meant for politicians, actors, and business elites.

She entered a grand corridor and paused.

The walls were lined with oil paintings—ancestors of the Diwan family, all staring down with self-importance. Crystal chandeliers dangled like frozen waterfalls. She began wiping surfaces with quick efficiency, but her mind wandered.

So many years had passed, yet this house still smelled the same—jasmine oil, cigar smoke, and power.

As she walked to get fresh water, her path took her behind the animal enclosures. Diwan Singh, a lover of rare dog breeds, kept a dozen of them in lavish kennels. Barking echoed in the stone corridor.

But what caught her attention wasn't the barking—it was silence.

In one of the shaded cells, she saw a man. Sitting inside a cage. Chained. His eyes were blank, staring ahead. His hair was long, and his face was partly hidden in shadows. She blinked.

Was this real?

She stepped closer.

His body was bruised in places. The chain was looped through a metal rod attached to the wall. A bowl of water sat near him, untouched.

Who was he?
A servant punished? A prisoner? A madman?

Before she could ask or look further, a loud voice rang out behind her.

"Don't wander! Get to work fast!" one of the guards shouted.

Radha turned and walked quickly back, but the image burned itself into her memory.

She didn't know why—but something about that man felt important.

As Radha dusted the furniture inside the west wing, old memories came uninvited—like angry ghosts.

She had survived. But she hadn't forgiven. Because of Mr. Diwan, Radha and Raju were separated.

And now, she was being forced to swallow every ounce of rage for the sake of one rented room and a factory job.

But one thought kept pulsing inside her: Who was that man in chains?

Why would someone be hidden like that in a mansion preparing for a celebration?

Was he a secret?

Or a warning?

She decided— she would try to find out. Lots of voices were asking people to hurry up. Radha also started walking fast to start the assignment. Her mind was loaded with thoughts as she was rushing.

✦✦✦

CHAPTER 12

THE ANNOUNCEMENT

The mansion was aglow with opulence. Soft golden lights shimmered over silk drapes. A crystal chandelier, imported from Italy, bathed the grand ballroom in luxury. The Diwans had spared no expense. Every detail of the party screamed grandeur—from the soft strains of classical violin at the entrance to the velvet-covered armchairs, and the marble-topped buffet counters laid with gold-plated cutlery.

Outside, a queue of imported luxury cars began pulling into the private driveway, each one greeted by valet staff dressed in royal blue sherwanis. The who's who of Madhya Pradesh stepped out—ministers, business tycoons, film personalities, bureaucrats, and party high-command officials.

Mr. Diwan Singh and Chandraprabha Singh stood at the entrance of the ballroom, personally greeting each guest with folded hands and air-kisses of familiarity.

Diwan Singh's black bandh-gala suit, complete with a ruby brooch, stood out among the crowd. His smile tonight was not just of celebration—it was a victor's smile, the look of a man who had conquered.

From a hidden corner near the service hallway, Radha, her mother, and a few others from the working staff stood silently. Their work was done for the evening, and now they were allowed to witness the event from a distance. Plates of leftover snacks were passed among them. Radha wasn't interested in the food.

She watched the crowd with wide eyes. The sheer scale of the party was overwhelming—live instrumental music, dance performances, speeches, and camera flashes going off every second.

Radha's gaze, however, kept drifting toward the people, not the glitz. The powerful faces, the knowing smirks, the casual corruption dressed in designer suits. She whispered to her mother, "They celebrate like kings."

Her mother replied quietly, "They are kings. This is their kingdom."

Suddenly, a line of black SUVs approached with flashing red beacons. The air shifted. The background music softened. A murmur passed through the crowd.

One of the staff hurried toward Mr. Diwan and whispered: "Shri Mahan Baba has arrived."

Diwan's face lit up. This was the moment he had been truly waiting for.

Mahan Baba, now Minister of Industrial Development. Had once been a spiritual figure with millions of followers. But politics had shaped him into something else—part godman, part kingmaker. His white robes were crisp, his bald head shining under the soft lights, and his eyes sharp as ever.

Diwan Singh and Chandraprabha rushed to welcome him, bowing slightly—not just out of respect, but strategic submission.

They led Mahan Baba to a plush armchair placed at the center of the VVIP row.

After a few moments, Mahan Baba leaned toward Diwan and whispered, "Your long-pending task is done. That 600-acre tribal land... It's now yours. We've reclassified it for industrial use."

He smiled, eyes twinkling with power. "You can begin your steel project. Allocation orders will be delivered to your office tomorrow. My PA will handle the rest."

Mr. Diwan's face was lit with a joy rarely seen on his usually guarded expression. It was the expression of a man who had finally seized his empire.

He stood up and whispered to a guard, "Call Chetan."

Chetan arrived promptly. Dressed in a sharp maroon jacket, he stood tall—but his eyes held questions. Diwan whispered something in his ear. Chetan's face registered mild surprise, then confusion.

He turned and walked briskly toward the stage area.

Soon after, the stage lights dimmed slightly. The emcee, dressed in glittering ethnic wear, stepped onto the stage with a bright smile.

"Ladies and gentlemen, a moment of silence and attention, please. We request Mr. Diwan Singh and his son, Mr. Dilip Diwan, to join us on stage for a very special announcement."

The crowd turned toward the stage, murmuring in curiosity. Dilip looked around, clearly startled.

He leaned toward his father, "Papa, what's going on?"

Diwan didn't answer. Just placed a firm hand on his back and guided him to the stage.

The applause was thunderous as they walked together. Chandraprabha looked on, her expression unreadable.

Diwan took the microphone. His voice, deep and authoritative, echoed through the massive hall.

"My dear friends and well-wishers, tonight is special—not just because my son has returned from abroad, but because I want to share something personal."

He paused for effect, scanning the crowd.

"It is every father's dream to see his son succeed. And today, I'm proud to say that my son, Dilip Diwan, has graduated from a prestigious university in France. He has returned not just with a degree, but with vision."

The crowd clapped politely.

Diwan continued, "Tonight, I also want to make a commitment—to this state, to our people. I'm announcing the creation of a Mega Steel Industrial Park. It will provide thousands of jobs and transform the region."

He smiled proudly.
"And this entire project will be headed by none other than Dilip."

A burst of applause followed.

Dilip, stunned, nodded awkwardly and waved at the crowd. He had no speech ready. This was not discussed. Not even hinted. Yet here he was—crowned, without consent.

As they stepped off the stage, well-wishers surrounded Dilip, showering him with praise and congratulations.

Flashbulbs popped. Selfies were taken. He barely heard the voices.

Inside, he was in turmoil.

In a quieter corner of the mansion, Chetan stood with Chandraprabha. His face, usually calculated, was now flushed with fury.

"You called me for this?" Chandraprabha asked.

Chetan didn't answer immediately. He was pacing.

Then he turned and said bitterly, "Do you really not know? For the last year, I've handled every detail of that tribal land project. The bribes. The threats. The paperwork. The press. Everything."

Chandraprabha stayed silent.

"And now," he continued, "the steel project is announced on stage—and the spotlight is given to Dilip? Just like that? I didn't even know he wanted to work here!"

"I know you're upset," she said, calming her tone. "But I will talk to Mr. Diwan. He trusts you. Maybe this was just… symbolic."

Chetan laughed darkly.

"Symbolic? You really believe that? You know how power works in this house."

Just then, some guests called from the hallway, "Chetan bhaiya! We're leaving."

He turned toward them and forced a smile. "Coming."

Before leaving, he turned to Chandraprabha and said quietly, "This isn't over. It's unfair."

Then he disappeared into the crowd.

Back in the ballroom, the party continued. Music resumed. Laughter floated. But in corners, conversations had changed.

Some were murmuring about the unexpected elevation of Dilip.
Some were wondering if Chetan had been sidelined.
Some simply watched Diwan and Mahan Baba with new respect—and fear.

And in a dimly lit corridor near the animal enclosures, Radha stood again, staring quietly at the locked cell where the man in chains sat.

She couldn't let go of what she had seen.

Something was deeply wrong in this house.

She could feel it.

✦✦✦

CHAPTER 13

THE MAN IN CHAINS

Once the last car had driven away and the lights on the stage dimmed, the mansion began to breathe again—not with celebration, but with fatigue. The orchestra had stopped playing. The servers slumped against the walls, stretching their legs. A few of the staff started gathering in the service area, where leftover food had been laid out for them.

Radha and her mother joined the others near the rear courtyard, where the buffet's remains still looked like a feast to those who could never afford one. There was pulao, creamy paneer, kofta curry, naan still warm, and rich gulab jamuns swimming in syrup.

"Eat as much as you can, Radha," her mother said, gently nudging her forward. "We don't get this kind of food every day."

Radha nodded silently and picked up a plate. But her eyes weren't on the food.

They were searching.

As she took a spoonful of rice, she saw him—the man from the cage.

He was sitting in the shadows of a side courtyard wall, hunched and quiet. A steel plate rested on his lap with a few plain rotis and dal. He ate with small, careful bites, as though food was a ritual, not a meal.

Curiosity tugged at Radha again. She handed her plate to her mother and quietly walked toward him.

He noticed her as she approached and gave a slow nod of acknowledgement, not warmth—just a gesture of recognition. His frame was fragile, his bones showing at the elbows, and his eyes were deeply sunken, but strangely calm. His hair was graying, and his beard was patchy. He looked like a man who had aged far ahead of his time.

Radha folded her hands slightly in greeting.
"Namaste, Baba."
He gave a faint nod in return. "Namaste."

They sat in silence for a moment, the noise of the rest of the staff like a distant background hum.

Then she asked quietly, "You were in that cell… the one with the dogs… chained. Why?"

The man stopped chewing. He looked at her carefully, eyes narrowing with suspicion—but there was no hostility.

After a pause, he answered in a low voice, "I chained myself."

Radha blinked, confused. "What? Why would you do that to yourself?"

"To atone for the sins of my son." His voice was quiet. "He is no longer in this world… but I remain."

A Story from the Shadows

The man leaned back against the wall, as if releasing a weight from his chest.

"My name is Ramlal, though no one here bothers to use it anymore. For over thirty years, I worked for the Diwan family. I was the caretaker of their animals—horses and dogs. I was given a servant quarter behind the kennels, near the stables. My whole world was there."

He paused, staring at the dust near his feet.

"My wife died when our son Sahil was only ten. From then on, it was just me and him. I raised him as best I could. He was bright—much smarter than I ever was. Loved animals, just like I did. I used to take him on the horses when he was a boy, let him play with the puppies in the kennels. That's where he met… her."

Radha knew without being told—Rajni Diwan.

"They were just children at first," Ramlal continued. "Playing, reading, laughing. She used to help him with schoolwork. Sahil went to the government school. Rajni, of course, had the best tutors. But she would come back from school, change, and sit with him in the garden. I used to smile, watching from the side, thinking what a blessing it was that my son had such a friend."

He paused. "A friend… until it turned into love."

"They grew up. Rajni joined an engineering college. So did Sahil—the same college. He cleared the entrance exams with high marks. I was so proud… we had nothing, but he had brains and will."

His voice began to quiver.

"But Mr. Diwan… he found out. He wasn't just angry. He was furious. Insulted. Humiliated. A girl from one of the richest and most powerful families in the state… and a boy who fed his dogs. It was not just love for him. It was defiance."

Ramlal's voice dropped even lower. "They beat my son. Mr. Diwan and his men. Sahil was pulled out of his hostel and thrashed. I begged—literally fell at Mr. Diwan's feet—to let him live. He agreed… on one condition."

He looked at Radha. "That Sahil would never again see Rajni. Never speak to her. Never come near her. I made Sahil swear it. And he did. For a year, he kept his promise. He finished college. He said he'd get a job and we'd start a new life. I believed him."

He stopped. His hands trembled as he held the edge of his plate.

"But love doesn't listen to oaths. A month after he graduated… they eloped."

Radha gasped softly.

"I was working the night shift at the kennel when I heard the news. And a few days later… I saw his body. My son… broken. Dead."

He looked away as if hiding his tears in the dark.

"No one ever spoke of Rajni after that. They said she had disgraced the family."

"Mr. Diwan called me one evening. Said killing me would be too easy. He told me, 'Let your caste see what happens when one of them dares touch one of us.' He told me to live in shame. To be an example."

And so I chained myself.

"Every morning for five years, I come to that cell. I put on the chain. Not locked by anyone else—I do it myself. Like a ritual. I sit there until the sun goes down. Then I go home."

"Why?" Radha whispered, tears threatening to rise. "Why punish yourself? You didn't do anything."

He gave a bitter smile. "A father's burden, child. When your son dies not just in body, but in honor… what else can a father do? I couldn't save him. I couldn't stop him. But maybe,just maybe— in this life, if I suffer enough, his soul will find peace."

Radha was silent for a long time.

Around them, the chatter of the staff continued. The moon had risen high. The animals had gone quiet. Only the occasional bark echoed from the kennels.

Radha wanted to say something—anything—but no words came.

Just then, her mother called out from a distance. "Radha, we have to go. The bus is waiting."

Radha nodded and looked at Ramlal. "Can I come talk to you again?"

He hesitated, then nodded. "If you're not afraid to talk to a ghost."

She smiled faintly. "Ghosts don't cry like you do."

As she walked back toward the bus, something inside her had changed. A story that was buried behind wealth and walls had come alive again. A cruel history masked by chandeliers and speeches. A grief that breathed from behind a dog's cage.

She looked back once and saw him sitting there.

Still.

Like a statue built from guilt.

Chained—but only on the outside.

✦✦✦

CHAPTER 14

THE CALM BEFORE FIRE

Pachmarhi – On the Sacred Banks of Narmada

The soft chants of temple bells echoed through the forests of Pachmarhi, mingling with the rhythmic flow of the Narmada River, which shimmered under the morning sun. Birds darted across the sky, and the scent of incense hung in the air. It was here, on these tranquil banks, that Rajendra Guru found his sanctuary.

An elderly priest stood near the ancient Shiva temple, waiting patiently at the carved entrance.

As Rajendra arrived, the priest greeted him with deep respect. "Aniket Guru informed me you'd be coming. All arrangements for your stay have been made."

He smiled warmly, folding his hands. "Fauji Baba is like a living god to us. Years ago, my wife was dying of cancer. The doctors gave us six months, said the waiting list for surgery was long. But one call from Fauji Baba to

Delhi… and the operation was done within a week. She is alive today because of him."

Rajendra bowed his head slightly, humbled by the gratitude.

The priest led him past the temple's sanctum to a small but peaceful room at the back. The room was simple—a bed, a cooler, a pitcher of water, and a window overlooking the flowing Narmada and the temple courtyard.

"You will find peace here, Guruji," the priest said, placing a clean bedsheet on the bed. "My wife will prepare your food. I will bring it daily. Our home is just behind the temple. You're not a guest—you are our blessing."

Rajendra gave a nod of gratitude.

"There is one more thing," the priest added. "Every morning, after mangal aarti, you may deliver your discourse to the devotees. A small stage has been built near the ghats. You may also meet followers privately afterward. I will make sure you are not disturbed."

Rajendra looked out the window, at the temple bells swinging in rhythm with the wind, at the wide expanse of the holy river.

"Thank you, Panditji. I will begin my duties from tomorrow."

The priest left him alone to rest.

That night, Rajendra lay still on the bed. The hum of crickets outside was the only sound. The silence here was not empty—it was sacred, like something waiting to speak. For the first time in weeks, he slept deeply.

From the very next morning, Rajendra started his daily spiritual practice.

The aarti began before sunrise—flames flickering in brass plates, conch shells blowing in unison. After the ceremony, Rajendra stood under a canopy near the ghats and spoke. His sermons were simple, laced with wisdom. He didn't preach miracles—he spoke of self-discipline, morality, and the balance between karma and justice.

What started as a handful of listeners grew week by week. Locals, travelers, small businessmen, retired officers, and even young students began gathering to listen.

Some came for peace. Some came with problems. Some just sit silently near the flowing river.

Every day, he gave time to individuals after the discourse—listening, advising, guiding.

Slowly, in the hills of Pachmarhi, a new circle of influence was forming.

Back at Diwan Mansion – The Tension Grows.

Meanwhile, in the heart of Bhopal, the Diwan mansion was stirring with a different kind of energy.

Chetan stood in the central study, holding a brown folder filled with stamped documents. "Uncle, I have good news. The paperwork for the tribal land is finalized. We can proceed. I've already asked the engineering team to do a preliminary site survey tomorrow."

Mr. Diwan smiled, taking the folder and flipping through the pages.

"Dilip, this is your project now," he said, turning to his son. "You decide how and what happens next. Chetan, make sure no decisions are made without Dilip's approval."

Chetan froze for a second. "Of course, uncle," he said, nodding stiffly.

Dilip stepped forward. "Thank you, Chetan. I appreciate your efforts. But before we send anyone, I want to visit the site myself. I want to see it, understand the surroundings, and decide the next steps. I also intend to form a separate engineering team—one dedicated purely to this project."

Mr. Diwan agreed. "A wise move. But don't go alone. The area is remote—take some of our men with you. Just for safety."

Chetan's jaw clenched slightly. This was not how it was supposed to be.

He had done the groundwork, made the calls, managed the shady transactions, even bribed the right officials to get the land cleared. And now he was expected to report to a man who barely understood the politics of business?

He kept his resentment buried, smiled politely, and nodded again.

But inside him, something was boiling.

Later that night, as the lights dimmed across the Diwan estate, Chetan sat alone in the veranda, swirling a glass of whisky.

His mind wasn't quiet.

He stared into the distance, murmuring to himself: "You think education makes you a leader, Dilip bhaiya? I'll show you what power really means."

In a remote ashram far away, Rajendra finished writing in his journal and closed his eyes, facing the Narmada. He was waiting for Aniket's next course of action.

✦✦✦

CHAPTER 15

THE LAND SPEAKS

The next morning, Dilip Diwan set out early for the site visit. The road to the land was rough,winding its way through the dense Satpura jungles. The rising sun filtered through the thick canopy, casting golden shadows on the dusty trail.

A convoy of three SUVs carried Dilip, his bodyguards, and aides. After four long hours, they finally reached the destination—a vast expanse of land, surrounded by lush green forests on three sides and scattered hamlets on the fourth.

Despite the fatigue, Dilip felt a strange connection to the place the moment he stepped out of the car. The fresh air, the rhythm of distant tribal drums, and the earthy silence—it was unlike anything he had experienced in his corporate upbringing.

A middle-aged man, wearing a white cotton turban and a dhoti, approached with folded hands.

"Namaste, Babuji. I am Kinchu Pradhan, head of the nearby village. A large part of land was once my family's... until the government took it, saying it was for a school and hospital. Now, we hear it's for a factory."

His tone was respectful, but his eyes carried the weight of loss.

Dilip shook his hand and asked to walk the land together. As they strolled, Kinchu shared how many in his village felt betrayed. The compensation received was far below expectations, and promises of welfare were never fulfilled.

Dilip listened carefully. This wasn't a boardroom negotiation—these were people's lives.

"Once the factory is up, I assure you—at least many members of your community will get jobs here. And we'll build a school too." Dilip said, offering what little he could in that moment.

Kinchu looked at him long and hard, then gave a slow nod. "We'll hold you to your word, babuji."

Dilip spent the rest of the afternoon sketching his vision. Though he was a businessman now, he had always loved art and drawing. On a rough sheet of paper, he outlined the plant's layout—the entrance, worker quarters, and green belt around the boundary.

This was more than a project. This was his chance.

On the way back, he felt light, excited. As he reached the mansion, he met his father and said, "Please get a date from our family priest for Bhoomi Puja. This project will be my life's work. From tomorrow, I'll begin forming the team."

Chetan, who had been sitting silently in a corner of the room, felt the sting of exclusion again. But Mr. Diwan sensed the air.

"Dilip, keep Chetan close. He's like your brother, and his experience will be useful. Let him be your partner."

Dilip nodded, though something in his gut felt uneasy.

The next day, Dilip visited Diwan Industries HQ, where he began handpicking his core team—engineers, legal advisors, and procurement heads. Chetan, trying to stay relevant, suggested names of a few loyal aides—men who had served the Diwan family for years.

Chetan also took charge of arranging the Bhoomi Puja, now set for next Thursday, a date chosen by the priest as most auspicious.

Everything was moving per plan.

Until the night before the puja.

Both Mr. and Mrs. Diwan fell sick—sudden high fever, body ache. The family doctor said it was likely a viral infection and advised rest.

Still, Mr. Diwan called Dilip to his room. "Don't cancel. Go ahead with the puja. It's a good omen for the project. Your mother and I will attend the inauguration when the factory is ready."

Dilip hesitated but agreed.

Early next morning, as the convoy was about to leave, Chetan's car broke down. Frustrated, he told Dilip to carry on and promised to join him shortly.

As the vehicles neared the project site, Dilip noticed a strange shift in energy. The road leading to the land was blocked by hundreds of villagers, shouting slogans.

He stepped out and turned to his security team.

"What's going on?"

One of the guards returned after speaking to a protester.

"Sir, they're shouting against Diwan Industries. Apparently, last night, statues of their village goddess emerged from different corners of the land. The villagers believe the land is sacred now. Kinchu Pradhan says he saw a dream—his forefathers told him this land belongs to Maa, and a grand temple must rise here."

"What nonsense!" Dilip snapped. "Where's Kinchu?"

He marched toward the crowd, flanked by his men. His heart was pounding—not in fear, but in anger.

"Kinchu! What's all this? You know this land is legally ours. This is a government allocation!"

Kinchu stepped forward. His face was calm, but his voice boomed.

"Law may say it is yours, but Dharma says otherwise. This land is no longer just land. Maa has chosen to appear. No industry will rise here now—only a temple."

Villagers roared in agreement.

Dilip tried reasoning. "We'll pay extra compensation. You can build the temple elsewhere. But don't halt development. This project is for everyone's future."

Kinchu didn't flinch.

"You can't buy faith with money, Babuji. And when Maa wants to dwell, no man can stop her."

The argument escalated. Emotions flared. Dilip, usually composed, lost control.

In a moment of rage, he grabbed Kinchu's collar, shouting, "Stop this madness!"

What followed was chaos.

The crowd surged forward. Shouting, pushing, hurling stones. Dilip's guards tried shielding him, but were outnumbered.

Just then, Chetan's car screeched to a halt. He stepped out, took stock of the chaos, and without a second thought, fired two rounds in the air from his revolver.

The gunshots stunned the crowd into silence.

Chetan raised both hands.

"Please! Please calm down! No one wants violence here. Dilip didn't mean harm. We promise no construction will begin until we all talk again. Please, forgive him."

He turned to Kinchu and folded his hands.

"We all make mistakes. Let's not let this become a tragedy."

Kinchu nodded slightly, signaling the villagers to step back.

Chetan immediately rushed to Dilip, whose shirt was torn, face scratched, and pride bruised.

They drove back in silence.

Back at the mansion, Mr. Diwan was livid. After listening to everything, he turned to Chetan.

“Thank you, beta. You saved my son today. Saved our name.”

Dilip sat quietly, humiliated.

“I told you not to go alone,” Mr. Diwan scolded. “This isn’t a college project, Dilip. These people don’t follow logic—they follow fear, emotion, tradition.”

He picked up the phone and called the Police Commissioner.

After a few minutes of conversation, he hung up.

“The Commissioner will handle it,” Mr. Diwan said. “But he’s warned us—no violence, no confrontation. We’ll let the administration calm things down. This could take weeks, even months.”

Mahan Baba has also been suddenly called to Delhi; it seems like he may get a post in the Cabinet. He has asked not to be disturbed. So, we need to be a bit patient.

The room went silent.

Chetan looked at Dilip, and for the first time in weeks, his smile returned.

✦✦✦

CHAPTER 16

THE COST OF DECEIT

The confrontation between Diwan Industries and the local villagers had made national news. The headlines screamed:

"Rural Resistance Halts Industrial Giant!"

"Sacred Land or Strategic Plot? Tempers Flare in Central India"

In the tranquil temple complex on the banks of the Narmada, Rajendra Guru sat cross-legged under a peepal tree, reading the newspaper. His eyes didn't widen, but the tension in his brow deepened.

Aniket Guru, his old mentor and spiritual guide, approached with measured steps.

"Now is your time, Rajendra. The land is restless, the people divided. Start visiting the surrounding villages. Speak to them. Heal them. Establish your presence."

Rajendra nodded. "Not as a leader, Guruji, but as a servant of truth."

One Month Later.

Word of Rajendra Guru's presence spread across villages like wildfire. Every morning, a few more people joined his prayers, attended his sermons. He listened patiently, offered simple wisdom, and healed more hearts than he knew.

Meanwhile, strange whispers floated in the air—Kinchu Pradhan, once seen as the torchbearer of resistance, had begun living a mysteriously lavish lifestyle. Villagers noted a shiny new refrigerator, a washing machine, and even a two-door almirah delivered to his humble house.

Questions lingered, but no one dared speak aloud.

One afternoon, Kinchu Pradhan was speeding down the highway on his old bike, humming a folk tune. The road was deserted—except for a black SUV that appeared from nowhere, hurtling down at breakneck speed.

There was no warning.

The car slammed into the bike with brutal force, tossing Kinchu into the air before speeding away, disappearing in a cloud of dust.

Blood pooled on the asphalt. Kinchu screamed, "Help! Help me!"

A few minutes later, Rajendra Guru's car was passing by. His driver slammed the brakes as they spotted the mangled body on the roadside.

Without hesitation, Rajendra stepped out, lifted Kinchu into the car, and rushed him to the district hospital.

The doctors worked quickly. Both of Kinchu's legs were fractured, and he'd lost a lot of blood. A nurse ran out, asking for an urgent B-positive donor.

"I'm B-positive," Rajendra said calmly. "Begin the transfusion."

Over the next few days, Rajendra visited Kinchu daily. He brought fruits, warm food, and sometimes just silent companionship.

One evening, as the sun dipped below the Narmada, Kinchu broke down.

"I will be forever indebted to you, Guruji. You saved my life."

Rajendra replied softly, "I am but an instrument. The will belongs to God."

Kinchu's lips trembled. "Guruji… this accident… It's not just fate. It's punishment. A curse from the Goddess. I misused Her name."

Rajendra listened, unmoving.

"A man came to me before the Bhoomi Pujan. He offered me a deal. He said, 'Stir up the villagers, create a divine story, make sure the Puja doesn't happen. Later, I'll help calm things down, and you'll get more money.' He gave me a handsome advance. I got greedy."

He looked down in shame.

"But now… now I've lost control. The people are too angry. Even if I want peace, they won't listen to me. I've started a fire I can't extinguish."

He covered his face and sobbed.

Rajendra stood, walked over to the bedside, and placed a gentle hand on Kinchu's head.

"Every man faces darkness. But it's what he does next that defines him."

He paused.

"Forget this deal. If that man contacts you again, say nothing. Delay him. Distract him. And about the villagers—leave them to me."

Kinchu looked up, eyes wide.

"You… you'll help them forgive me?"

"I'll help them see the truth, and leave the rest to the Goddess."

With a final blessing, Rajendra turned and walked out of the hospital room, his saffron robes brushing the cold floor, his mind already charting the next step in this quiet war between faith and greed.

✦✦✦

CHAPTER 17

BLOODLINES AND SHADOWS

It was a cool evening at the Diwan Mansion. The sky above Bhopal was flushed with a warm orange hue as the sun began to set. In the quiet corner of the sprawling veranda, Chandraprabha Singh handed a steaming cup of tea to Mr. Diwan, who was lost in the garden's silence.

"Tea," she said softly.

Mr. Diwan took the cup, inhaled the aroma, and looked at her knowingly. "You want to say something."

Chandraprabha hesitated. "Yes… I've been thinking. I know you want Dilip to take responsibility, but… don't you think this project might be too much for him, especially as his first real assignment?"

Mr. Diwan raised an eyebrow. "He needs to learn. How long will we keep him sheltered?"

"I agree," she said. "But he's still young. This land issue has been dragging on for two months now. The villagers won't budge. He's trying hard, but what if he fails? It might break his confidence. Why not shift him to internal operations—finance, marketing? Let Chetan handle the land and factory construction. He's got experience, knows how to deal with pressure and people."

Mr. Diwan took a slow sip of his tea. "Chetan has always been loyal. A great man. Sometimes, I think… if only he had been my son."

Chandraprabha gave a faint smile. "He *is* like your son."

"But not *my* son," Mr. Diwan said, his voice sharper. "He doesn't have my blood. It was your father who insisted I take him in when he was ten. I didn't even know the boy. You told me he was the orphaned son of someone close to your father, killed in a car accident. That's all I know."

Chandraprabha looked away, her voice barely above a whisper. "Does the blood really matter, after all he's done for you?"

"I'm not denying his loyalty or intelligence," Mr. Diwan said. "He's capable. If Dilip weren't in the picture, I might have even considered handing the reins of the business to him."

Chandraprabha gave a weak laugh. "Seems you love him more than our own son."

Mr. Diwan chuckled. "Maybe. Let's see… maybe I will give him more responsibility."

Later That Night.

The mansion was quiet. Servants had retired to their quarters. The air was still, except for the chirping of distant crickets. Chandraprabha walked down the corridor, hesitated outside Chetan's room, then knocked softly.

Chetan opened the door and smiled. "Come in, Aunty."

She stepped in, locked the door behind her. Turning to him, her eyes softened. "There's no one here… you can call me Mummy."

Chetan's expression shifted. "Okay, Mummy… did you talk to Uncle?"

"I did. I've been trying to convince him. I think he'll change his mind soon. Just give it a few more days." She stepped closer. "You must make him feel like you'd do *anything* for him. That's the key."

"I will. I promise," Chetan said.

Then, after a pause, he asked gently, "Can I ask something, Mummy? Do you love me… or Dilip more?"

Her eyes moistened. She turned away for a moment. “What kind of question is that? For a mother, all children are equal…”

She paused, her voice trembling.

“…But you… you are the son of my *first love*.”

Chetan stood frozen.

“I still remember,” she continued. “Your father and I… we eloped. We ran away to Shimla. We were so happy. We didn’t tell anyone, not even my family. Then that car accident… it took everything. I was pregnant with you. My father found me… brought me back… forced me to hide everything. To this day, not even Diwan knows the truth. He believes you’re the son of a family friend.”

Tears rolled down her cheeks. “I could never give you your true identity, never let you call me ‘Maa’ in public. That guilt has eaten me alive for over twenty-five years.”

Chetan’s eyes were wide with emotion. “Mummy…”

She held his hands, trembling. “You are my son. No matter what the world believes. Never forget that.”

Chetan didn’t speak. He simply knelt, placed his head in her lap, and let her stroke his hair in silence—a mother’s love breaking through years of secrecy.

Outside, the wind rustled the leaves of the neem tree. Inside, something sacred had been spoken—something that would change destinities.

✦✦✦

CHAPTER 18

THE RISING STORM

A man called Chetan on the phone.

"Sir… Kinchu has been in the hospital for several days now. Both his legs are fractured. He's refusing to fulfill the promise—he won't convince the villagers."

Chetan's voice was sharp. "We need to make him fall in line. Once he cooperates, I'll have full control over the land and the factory project."

"I'll try again, Sir," the man responded meekly.

There was a brief pause on the line. Then Chetan spoke again, cold and decisive.
"Forget it. I'll handle him myself."

Within the hour, Chetan was in his car with a few of his trusted men. They headed straight to the district hospital.

Inside the hospital, Chetan walked briskly through the corridor, ignoring nurses and staff trying to stop him. His men shoved aside anyone who got in their way. Within moments, they reached Kinchu's ward.

The village head lay weakly on the bed, both legs in plaster, his face pale and bruised. He looked up in alarm as Chetan entered, flanked by men holding guns discreetly at their sides.

Chetan stepped close to the bed, his tone ice-cold.

"Let me come straight to the point. I'm Mr. Diwan's nephew. You know that already. Whatever wealth you've been flaunting lately… It'sbecause of me. Don't forget who made that possible."

"I understand, sir," Kinchu replied softly. "But…"

"But what?" Chetan snapped, cutting him off.

"The situation has changed. The villagers— they won't listen to me anymore. The protests have taken a life of their own."

"Don't give me excuses. If you want, you *can* convince them," Chetan said, his voice rising.

Then he leaned closer, his expression menacing. "You like the idea of a bullet through your chest? One signal from me and you're gone."

Kinchu folded his hands, trembling. "Sir, please… forgive me. I swear, I tried. But it's beyond me now. The people have turned deeply emotional. They believe the goddess has claimed that land. They won't listen."

He paused, hesitating, then added, "There's one person who might help… Rajendra Guru. He teaches at the Shiva Temple in Panchgarhi. He visits our village often. The people trust him. They listen to him like he's divine."

Chetan narrowed his eyes. "And if *he* fails to convince them?"

Kinchu looked away, silently.

Chetan gave a cold smile.
"Then rest assured—six bullets will kiss your heart."

With that, he stormed out of the ward. On his way out, he turned to one of his men.

"Find out everything you can about this Rajendra Guru. We're going to meet him tomorrow."

Elsewhere in Bhopal, in a sleek, upscale café, Dilip was sitting across from an old college friend, sipping coffee in silence.

"You look low, man. What's bothering you?" the friend asked.

Dilip gave a half-hearted shrug. "Dad asked me to let Chetan handle the mega factory project. It was supposed to be my chance to prove myself… and now it's gone."

His friend leaned forward. "Don't take it so hard. You still have time. Trust yourself—you'll bounce back. By the way, remember Panchgarhi Shiva Temple? We used to bike there often in college."

Dilip smiled faintly. "Yeah, good times."

"There's a baba staying there now—Rajendra Guru. My mother was unwell for months. Doctors couldn't help. She met him once… and her health turned around. I know you don't really believe in these things, but… maybe it's worth a visit?"

Dilip sighed. "You know I don't buy into all this god-man stuff."

"I get it. But no harm in riding out there. If nothing else, we'll get some fresh air and relive our old days."

After a moment's pause, Dilip smiled and nodded. "Alright. Let's go tomorrow morning. Let's meet this baba—who knows, maybe he *can* fix my problem."

The two friends laughed, clinking their coffee cups, unaware that their lives were about to change.

✦✦✦

CHAPTER 19

MASKS AND MOTIVES

Radha sat quietly in a corner of her small room, immersed in drawing. Art had always been her escape and her expression. She had an uncanny ability to visualize people's appearances—even projecting how someone might look in the future or looked in past. Her talent had made her popular in the *mohalla*; children, women, even local shopkeepers often came to her with requests for personalized sketches.

As she put the finishing touches on her latest drawing, she glanced at a newspaper clipping pinned beside her desk. It showed a picture of Rajendra Guru standing beside Kinchu in a hospital bed, under the headline:

"Spiritual Guru Saves Village Leader from Death"

Radha had brought the clipping from her office, intrigued by the photo. Something about the face of the spiritual guru had stayed with her. She held her sketch beside the clipping. Her heart skipped a beat.

"He looks just like Raju..." she whispered. "I must meet him... just once... to know for sure."

At the Shiva Temple in Panchgarhi, morning rituals had begun. After leading the *aarti* and delivering his daily discourse, Rajendra Guru started receiving the usual stream of villagers, each seeking guidance, blessings, or solace.

Among the queue of visitors, a temple volunteer approached him and whispered, "Baba, *Dilip Diwan*, heir of the Diwan Group, has come to meet you."

Rajendra nodded. "Let him wait a little. I'll meet him after these people are done."

When the crowd had thinned, Dilip and his friend were ushered in. They respectfully greeted Rajendra, who raised his hand in blessing and motioned them to sit.

Dilip spoke earnestly. "Baba, I've come to seek your help. There's a major issue with land acquisition for our factory project. The villagers are angry, and nothing I try seems to work. I was told you have deep influence in the area. Could you help mediate a solution?"

Rajendra replied calmly, "I do not interfere directly in worldly matters. I only guide people in the right direction."

"But Baba," Dilip pressed gently, "your words carry weight with the villagers. A single statement from you could resolve this. Please, I'm asking you for your help—not for me, but for progress and harmony."

Rajendra paused for a moment, thinking. Then he said, "I will try something. But only on one condition—you must do something meaningful for the villagers and this ashram."

"Of course. Tell me what you need," Dilip said sincerely.

"Help build a higher secondary school for the village children, and fund an ashram for *Shri Fauji Baba* on nearby land."

"That much, I can certainly do," Dilip replied.

"Then rest assured, your path will be cleared. But remember—your commitment must be true. No turning back."

"I promise, Baba. I'll handle it personally."

With a respectful bow, Dilip and his friend took their leave. Rajendra watched them go, then turned toward his room to rest.

Just as he reached the corridor, a new voice echoed.

"Baba! One moment…"

Chetan entered with a group of sharp-eyed men, their posture stiff, their presence loud. They greeted Rajendra with false smiles.

"The meeting time is over," Rajendra said calmly. "You'll have to return tomorrow."

"You don't know who I am," Chetan replied, raising his chin. "I'm *Chetan Diwan*—nephew of the great industrialist, Mr. Diwan."

Then, in a quieter voice, he added, "I waited until Dilip left before stepping in."

Rajendra raised an eyebrow. "I've already met your brother. What more is there to say?"

"I'm here to ensure you *don't* act on anything he said. You'll wait for *my* direction—and only then will you speak to the villagers."

"I've already given my word to your brother," Rajendra said firmly.

"Words mean nothing," Chetan sneered. He slowly pulled out a pistol from his coat. "Guns change everything."

Rajendra remained calm. "You may threaten me, but I don't fear weapons."

"You may not," Chetan said coldly, pointing the gun toward the temple priest sitting nearby, blissfully unaware. "But others around you are vulnerable. I'd hate for someone innocent to bleed."

Rajendra's eyes narrowed. "There's no need for violence. Perhaps we can work out something."

Chetan smirked. "My brother offered to build a school and an ashram. I'll build *two*. Just make sure the credit for resolving the land issue goes *only* to me. Not to Dilip. Understood?"

Rajendra took a deep breath. "Fine. Give me two days. I'll think about it."

"You have exactly two days," Chetan repeated. "And don't you dare help Dilip."

Rajendra nodded silently. Chetan holstered his weapon and left with his men.

Later that evening, Rajendra sat in his modest room, thinking over the whirlwind of the day. He picked up his phone and called Aniket.

After listening to Rajendra's account, Aniket chuckled.

"Good. Everything is going as per the plan. You're close—very close—to settling the old score with Mr. Diwan."

Rajendra frowned. "What plan? I'm not sure where this is heading."

Aniket's voice was cryptic. "Let it unfold. You'll know when the time is right."

After the call, Rajendra lay on his cot, preparing for a short nap. Just as his eyes began to close, there was a soft *knock* at the door.

His eyes opened.

"Who could it be now?" he thought, as he rose to answer the knock, unaware that the next visitor might change everything.

✦✦✦

CHAPTER 20

THE KNOCK OF THE PAST

There was a soft knock on the wooden door of the room.

Rajendra Guru, still reclining from a brief rest, sat up slowly. The day's conversations were still echoing in his mind — Dilip's earnest request, Chetan's threats, Aniket's cryptic words. But something about this knock felt different. Gentle. Hesitant.

He opened the door.

A young woman stood before him, her head bowed respectfully, palms joined in greeting.

"Who are you?" Rajendra asked, with a tone of calm curiosity. "I usually don't meet anyone after lunch. How did you even get past the temple staff? They don't let people in at this hour."

She raised her eyes—soft, familiar eyes that seemed to tremble with unspoken emotion.

“Forgive me, Gurudev,” she said quietly. “I told them… I told them that you’ve known me for a long time. That you were expecting me.”

Rajendra’s brows furrowed.

“I have something urgent to show you. Please… may I come in? Just for a moment.”

There was something in her voice that caught him off guard. Familiar. Fragile.

He took a deep breath and stepped aside. “Come in.”

She entered slowly, carefully, like someone crossing a threshold not just into a room but into the pages of her own past. Rajendra offered her a seat.

She sat, silently reaching into her cloth bag. With gentle care, she took out four hand-drawn portraits, laying them on the floor in front of him.

The first showed a teenage boy, around fifteen, with mischievous eyes, messy hair.
The second, slightly older Eighteen , leaner face, traces of determination.
The third showed him clean-shaven, matured.
And the fourth—the one that stilled Rajendra’s breath—was a bearded figure, eyes calm, composed.
His current self.

Next to it, she placed a newspaper clipping showing *Rajendra Guru* with Kinchu at the hospital.

Rajendra stared in disbelief.

His voice cracked. "Radha… Are you… Are you *Radha*?"

Her eyes welled up. She nodded.

For a long moment, neither of them spoke. Words were unnecessary—tears, glances, and silence carried more weight than any language could.

"I searched for you," Rajendra whispered. "For years. But you had vanished without a trace. I thought… I thought I'd lost you forever."

Radha's lips trembled. "When you were arrested… when they said you were in jail… one of Mr. Diwan's men came. He offered my mother money—enough to survive. In return, she had to testify against you. She agreed… she was afraid."

Rajendra clenched his fists, but then released them slowly. "You don't need to explain, Radha. I understand. She was protecting you."

"They took us away from the street after a few days," Radha continued. "We were moved to Bhopal. My mother was given the job of cleaning floors at one of

Mr. Diwan's factories. I was too young then, but two years ago I started working in the canteen. Life is simple, but heavy."

She paused, her gaze dropping to the newspaper clipping.

"Last week, someone left this newspaper on a canteen table. When I saw your photo, my heart skipped. I couldn't believe it. I took the clipping, came home, and started drawing. One after another, I kept sketching you—as I remembered you, and how I imagined you now. Then I compared it to the photo."

Rajendra listened, unmoving, lost in her voice.

"I was afraid to come," she continued. "But something told me… I had to know. I had to see if it was really you."

"I missed you, Radha," Rajendra said, his voice thick. "More than I can ever put into words. But even back then, I knew your name might put you in danger. That's why I never searched too loudly."

Radha nodded. "They warned us never to speak your name. Not to tell anyone where we came from, or who we knew. We were silenced..."

Then, as if time folded back on itself, they started talking—truly talking. About their lost childhood. About the life on the street in Delhi. About the day he left. About the years in between.

Rajendra shared his transformation from Raju, a boy wronged, to Rajendra Guru, a spiritual guide. His journey through isolation, pain, and finally, peace.

Radha told him about Bhopal—her struggles, her sketches, the lonely hours spent wondering what became of her only true friend.

Hours passed like minutes. Laughter mixed with tears. Two souls, long torn apart, were stitching their bond back together, thread by thread.

Eventually, Radha glanced out the window. Dusk had turned into night.

"I should go," she said reluctantly, gathering her drawings. "If I'm late, my mother will panic. She's still fearful… and strict."

She paused at the doorway. "Will you… Will you call me? Can we meet again?"

Rajendra gave a soft smile. "Of course, Radha. This time, we won't lose each other again."

She smiled, eyes shimmering with quiet joy. "Good night, Raju."

"Good night, Radha," he replied.

And as the door closed gently behind her, Rajendra sat back down, heart pounding not with conflict or fear—but with the overwhelming warmth of *home rediscovered.*

✦✦✦

CHAPTER 21

A SPARK IN THE SHADOWS

That night, Rajendra Guru could barely contain his excitement. The moment Radha had left his room, he rushed to his writing desk, picked up phone and dialed a number engraved in memory.

It rang once. Twice.

"Hello?" came the low, steady voice of Aniket Guru.

"Aniket Guru," Rajendra's voice was brimming with emotion. "It's me."

"I know. I was expecting your call," Aniket said. "You sound… different."

"I found her, Aniket. *Radha*. She's alive. She came to see me today."

There was a pause on the line, and then a slow, knowing exhale from Aniket. "So the wheel of fate has finally turned."

Rajendra stood by the window, looking at the temple courtyard bathed in moonlight. His heart still fluttered from the reunion.

"I feel like… like my journey is complete," he said quietly. "As if all these years, all this pain, have led to this moment. To her."

"I'm happy for you, Rajendra. Truly," Aniket replied, but his tone turned firm. "But don't forget your path, don't let emotion make you abandon your purpose."

"Purpose?" Rajendra's tone softened. "Aniket… I've been thinking. What good is revenge? It may bring momentary satisfaction—but it's a cycle that never ends. I have Radha now. Perhaps that's enough."

There was silence for a few seconds, and then Aniket's voice sharpened with passion.

"No, Rajendra. This isn't just about you and Radha. It never was. If people like Mr. Diwan aren't held accountable, then others will continue to believe it's acceptable to sell, silence, or bury their daughters. What happened to Radha— to you— to so many others—cannot go unanswered."

Rajendra closed his eyes.

Aniket's voice softened slightly. "And perhaps Radha can be part of this. You said she works in one of Mr. Diwan's factories, right?"

"Yes."

"If she can somehow get closer… maybe even inside Diwan's mansion… it would help us more than you know."

"I don't want to risk her," Rajendra said, conflicted.

"Sometimes the only way to defeat darkness— is to walk through it together," Aniket said. "Talk to her Let her decide."

Rajendra nodded to himself. "I'll speak to her tomorrow."

Later That Week – Diwan Industries, Golden Jubilee Day

The factory grounds of Diwan Industries buzzed with unusual energy. Banners fluttered. Sweets were being distributed. A stage was set up with golden letters: *50 Years of Legacy – Diwan Group.*

Inside the staff quarters, Radha stood in front of the small mirror fixed to her locker. She had worn her best kurti—sky blue with white embroidery—and tied her hair into a neat braid. She pressed her lips together, nervous but composed. Today was a special day: Mr. Dilip Diwan himself was visiting the factory for the Golden Jubilee celebration.

Earlier that morning, the manager had pulled her aside.

"Radha, be ready early. Wear something neat. Press your clothes. Mr. Dilip will be meeting workers after lunch, and the canteen must be spotless."

Now, as the event unfolded, the sounds of speeches and applause echoed from the stage. Dilip Diwan arrived in a crisp grey suit, radiating charm and poise. After addressing the crowd, shaking hands with senior staff, and taking photos, he made his way to the canteen for a meal prepared by the workers.

The food was simple but delicious—fragrant dal, hot puris, and a sweet Radha had made herself. Dilip smiled with satisfaction. "The food here is better than what I get at home," he joked.

As he stood near the counter, the canteen manager began introducing the kitchen staff one by one. Then came Radha's turn.

"Sir, this is Radha," the manager said.

Radha stepped forward and handed him a rolled-up paper, her hands slightly trembling.

"I made something for you, sir," she said quietly.

Dilip raised an eyebrow. "Thank you. But what is it?"

"Please open it," she said, unable to hide her nervous smile.

He unrolled the paper carefully—and gasped in surprise.

It was a portrait series—five vivid pencil sketches of himself, showing different stages of life. As a child, one during adolescence, one in early adulthood One in college, and the final one—his current self in a suit and tie, standing confidently.

Each sketch was rich in detail. The contours of his jaw, the shifting expressions with age, the glint of ambition in his eyes—they were all there, captured beautifully.

"This is… incredible," Dilip said, genuinely amazed. "How did you manage to draw this so perfectly?"

"Just… from imagination," Radha replied with a small smile. "I've seen you in pictures around the factory. I just filled in the rest."

"You've got real talent," Dilip said. "Not just as an artist—but I hear you're a fantastic cook, too."

"She is, sir," the manager chimed in. "She makes the best food in this whole canteen."

"Well, then," Dilip said, thinking aloud, "our mansion cook is on leave for a few weeks. We could use someone like her there."

He turned to the manager. "Can you arrange for her to work at the house temporarily? Ensure all formalities are done."

The manager nodded.

Radha's eyes widened for a split second—but she managed to steady herself. This was happening. Just as Aniket had hoped.

"Thank you, sir," she said, bowing slightly. "I'll do my best."

Dilip smiled. "I'm sure you will."

As he walked away, chatting with the factory heads, Radha stood in silence, gripping the now-empty paper roll. Her heart beat fast—not with fear, but with purpose.

From a quiet artist in the canteen to a silent force inside the lion's den, Radha had stepped onto the stage of destiny.

✦✦✦

CHAPTER 22

MASKS AND SHADOWS

The temple courtyard shimmered in the late afternoon light, the scent of incense wafting from the sanctum where Rajendra Guru had just finished his evening discourse. Devotees were quietly dispersing, whispering blessings and bowing as they passed the Guru seated cross-legged on the temple platform.

But Rajendra's focus wasn't on the devotees.

His eyes were fixed on two unfamiliar men loitering near the temple gate, pretending to read donation boards and watching the inner sanctum too closely. One was chewing paan and looking around nervously, the other stood with arms folded, trying to blend in—unsuccessfully.

"They're not here to pray," Rajendra muttered under his breath. His instincts, long sharpened by hardship and experience, told him exactly who had sent them.

Chetan.

After the last devotee left, Rajendra walked slowly back to his quarters and immediately picked up his phone. He dialed Aniket.

"Chetan's men are here," he said without greeting. "They've been snooping around since morning. Looks like he's put me under watch."

"Of course he has," Aniket replied calmly. "He's a frightened man pretending to be powerful. We've disturbed his illusion of control. And frightened men, act recklessly."

"But he warned me, Aniket. He said I must obey him, or it won't be good. How should I respond?"

"Don't worry, Rajendra," Aniket said, his tone steady. "Let the drama between Dilip and Chetan stretch longer. The more it drags, the more tangled they get."

"How do we do that without getting crushed in between?" Rajendra asked.

"I've sent you something. Check your phone."

Rajendra unlocked his old but sturdy phone. A message from Aniket blinked—a video file.

He pressed play.

It was a clear recording of Chetan in his earlier visit to the temple. The video showed Chetan raising his gun, issuing threats, pacing angrily in front of Rajendra, the words sharp and dangerous.

Rajendra blinked. "How… how did you get this recorded?"

"I anticipated something might happen," Aniket said, almost smugly. "I asked one of the temple staff to keep his camera rolling from behind the curtain."

Rajendra exhaled slowly. "Even without coming here, you seem to have eyes everywhere."

Aniket chuckled. "Faith can be blind, but strategy must always see. We can use this video—but not yet. One piece of evidence is never enough. We gather more… and then we strike."

"Understood," Rajendra said. "But what do I tell them in the meantime? Chetan wants me to publicly support him. Dilip, on the other hand, is expecting me to side with him."

"Then give Chetan hope. Tell him you agree, but need time to convince the villagers. That will pacify him."

"And Dilip?"

"For him… give a ridiculous suggestion. Something symbolic but impossible. Tell him the villagers want him and his father to come to the village and fall at their feet to show humility. It will never happen. But it buys time."

Rajendra smiled slightly. "You really do think five moves ahead."

"That's how you win against men who've been kings for too long," Aniket said. "Trust the game."

Meanwhile, in the Diwan Mansion.

The Diwan mansion stood like a fortress of opulence—grand, cold, and intimidating. Marble lions guarded the gates. Long corridors whispered secrets of old wealth. Gilded chandeliers sparkled under silent ceilings. For most, the place was a symbol of power. But for Radha, it was the enemy's territory.

Her first few days were hard.

Chandra Prabha Singh, the stern matriarch of the Diwan family, ruled the mansion like a royal queen. She had strict rules—everything from how vegetables should be cut to which spices were allowed on certain days.

"The taste must be exact," she had warned Radha on the first day. "This is not a roadside eatery."

But Radha was resilient. She rose before dawn, bathed in cold water, prayed silently for strength, and devoted herself to the kitchen. She observed. She listened. And soon, her food began to speak for her.

Within days, murmurs began in the house.

"The new girl's vegetable curry tastes much better than the old cook's."

Even Chandra Prabha Singh, who rarely gave praise, simply said, "At least this one knows how to hold a spoon."

Radha smiled quietly when she heard it.

But her mission was not only in the kitchen.

Every late afternoon, she made time to visit the old man in chains, whom she had met during the Diwan party. His name was Ramlal.

He remains in dog quarters, in a small, filthy enclosure. His beard had grown long and wild, but his eyes still sparkled with intelligence. He was clearly someone once important—and now discarded like trash.

"Baba," she would call him softly.

At first, he didn't respond. Then one day, she brought him warm roti and milk. He looked up, startled.

"No one brings food for me," he said with cracked lips.

"I will," she promised.

Over the days, he began to speak.

Of how he had once worked for Mr. Diwan.

Of how he had seen men come and disappear.

Of how he had heard things—whispers behind closed doors, land grabbed by cheating, deals sealed with threats.

Radha listened silently, storing every word like gold coins, trying to get more insight into Diwan's life.

She was inside the mansion now. And the walls had started talking.

Every night, she used to send all the information gathered to Rajendra Guru.

✦✦✦

CHAPTER 23

A WHISPER BEHIND THE WALL

The monsoon clouds loomed heavy over Bhopal, turning the late morning into a hazy twilight. Thunder rumbled in the distance as Radha stirred the large iron pot of lentils inside the mansion's kitchen. The smell of spices and roasting onions hung thick in the air. Steam rose in clouds, fogging the brass lids and blurring the outlines of the cooks bustling around her.

Radha's mind was elsewhere.

She had been quietly gathering bits and pieces about the Diwan household—names, routines, whispers passed between servants. But so far, most of what she heard was surface-level. Gossip. Predictable.

She wanted more, Something real— Something that Rajendra and Aniket Guru could actually use.

Then, opportunity knocked—in the form of a command.

"Radha," barked the head cook, "today's lunch is for fifty people. Diwan Saab is sending food to the orphanage near Raisen Road. Chandraprabha Madam says it must be packed and ready in an hour."

Radha nodded without protest. She had learned long ago that resistance got you nowhere in the Diwan estate. Quiet efficiency, however, often earned your access.

The preparations began. Cauldrons of rice were set to boil; crates of vegetables were chopped. Radha moved swiftly, leading the effort without needing to speak.

Then, just as she was seasoning the final kadhai of aloo gobhi, a sudden gust of rose perfume reached her nose—a signature scent. She turned slightly.

Chandraprabha Singh had entered the kitchen.

She was dressed in a rust-orange silk sari, embroidered in gold, her temple jewelry already adorning her wrists and neck. Her forehead bore a fresh tilak, and her sharp eyes surveyed the room like a commander inspecting her troops.

"How much longer?" she asked crisply.

"Fifteen minutes," Radha replied, wiping her hands.

"Hurry up. We leave soon," Chandraprabha said, and then, curiously, lingered. Her gaze drifted across the burners, pausing briefly on Radha. Then, with a curt nod, she turned and walked out.

Radha watched her leave—and something in the way Chandraprabha moved, brisk but purposeful, lit a spark of suspicion.

She wasn't headed toward the car porch. Her feet turned toward the inner wing of the mansion—the older part, rarely used now except by a few key family members.

Radha leaned over to one of the other cooks. "Please keep an eye on the rice. I need a quick wash."

Without waiting for a response, she untied her apron and slipped into the narrow servant hallway.

She moved quickly but silently, her soft-soled slippers muffling every step.

Chandraprabha was just ahead, unaware she was being followed.

The path she took led to Chetan's room.

Radha's heartbeat quickened.

She crept up to the side corridor and stopped near a decorative wall that shared space with Chetan's quarters. This corner of the house was rarely patrolled by staff. It was dim, quiet… and perfect.

Radha pressed her ear against the cool plaster.

Inside, voices.

"Get up, Chetan. It's your father's death anniversary. We need to go to the orphanage to donate food and clothes, like every year."

It was Chandraprabha's voice—sharp, commanding, with a brittle edge.

A groggy murmur followed. Chetan, still in sleep's clutches, mumbled, "Let me sleep two more minutes, Ma…"

Radha's eyes widened.

Ma?

Chandraprabha snapped, "If you don't go, I'll go myself. I cannot miss my first husband's death anniversary."

"Okay, okay," Chetan grumbled. "I'll get up."

"Be quick and come down once you're ready," she said, and Radha heard footsteps approaching.

Panic surged. Radha dashed down the side hallway and slipped behind a pillar just as Chandraprabha emerged from the room. She didn't look back.

Radha exhaled in disbelief.

Chetan… is Chandraprabha's son? From her first marriage?

And—most shockingly—Mr. Diwan didn't know?

She stood there for a moment, stunned, before retracing her steps to the kitchen. Her hands moved by habit, finishing the remaining cooking as her mind turned over the revelation again and again.

Minutes later, staff members began loading the food into silver containers, wrapping them in cloth, and securing them in the back of the mansion's jeep.

Chetan appeared—dressed crisply, his hair still damp. He approached the vehicle with a forced smile.

"Ready, aunty?" he asked.

Radha, watching from the shadows of the veranda, couldn't believe the performance.

Chandraprabha simply nodded and stepped into the jeep.

From the lawn, Mr. Diwan sat under a parasol, sipping his tea, his newspaper open before him.

He glanced up, watching the jeep roll away.

"Don't know why these women have to overdo their temple routines," he muttered into his cup.

Radha didn't wait a second longer. She rushed to the servant quarters and fished out her phone. With trembling fingers, she dialed.

Rajendra answered immediately.

"Radha? Is everything alright?"

"I found something. A big one."

She whispered the entire conversation she had overheard. Rajendra remained silent for a few seconds.

Then: "Are you sure?"

"Yes. I heard it myself. Chetan called her *Maa*. Chandraprabha spoke about her first husband. Mr. Diwan doesn't know. It's huge."

There was a crackle on the line. Then came Rajendra's voice again, this time with electric excitement.

"This… these change everything. This is the crack we needed."

Within minutes, Rajendra called Aniket Guru and relayed the discovery. Aniket's voice was calm, but pleased.

"The puzzle is coming together," he said. "Let them turn against each other. Destiny doesn't need our help—only our patience."

"But this could get dangerous," Rajendra cautioned.

Aniket's voice didn't waver. "Don't worry. We'll guide it from the shadows. Like wind shaping a fire."

Then, almost as an afterthought, Aniket added, "By the way, three days from now—it's the annual celebration at Fauji Baba's ashram. It's his birthday too. He has asked to see both of you. Can you come?"

Rajendra's voice softened. "Of course. I'll speak to Radha. We'll be there."

"I'll arrange everything," Aniket promised. "Tell her… she's done well."

As Radha stood by the courtyard, the kitchen smells now fading into the breeze, her eyes scanned the horizon.

She had heard the whisper behind the wall.

And now, the game had changed.

✦✦✦

CHAPTER 24

A FACE FROM THE FRAME

The flight from Bhopal to Delhi had been quiet.

Not because there was nothing to say, but because sometimes, silence carries more weight than conversation. Rajendra and Radha sat beside each other, watching the clouds shift like restless memories outside the window. Occasionally, their hands would brush, and one of them would look up—just long enough to wonder if the other remembered everything too.

They both did.

As their taxi pulled out of the airport and merged onto the highway toward Fauji Baba's ashram, the city outside seemed both familiar and foreign. Delhi hadn't changed. But they had.

The dusty corners near Hanuman Mandir. The cracked pavement in front of the cinema where they once sat with beating hearts. The metro station that still bore the echo of their teenage laughter. It all passed like a montage of a former life.

Rajendra leaned slightly toward the window, his voice quiet.

"Do you remember... that day we ran all the way from Connaught Place to the temple, just to catch the last free meal?"

Radha smiled softly. "And then you gave your halwa to that old man. You said sweetness should be shared with those who've forgotten it."

He looked at her. "And you scolded me for it all the way back."

Their eyes met for a second too long. Then both looked away, their cheeks carrying secrets unspoken.

Fauji Baba's ashram had been transformed.

White canopies stretched over the wide courtyard, strings of marigold and jasmine fluttered in the breeze, and devotional music played on soft speakers tucked under neem trees. Saffron flags waved gently, and hundreds of devotees—sadhus, bureaucrats, businessmen, villagers—stood in queues holding garlands and fruits, waiting for a moment with the spiritual giant.

It looked less like an ashram and more like a royal court.

Rajendra and Radha stepped out of the taxi, joined by Aniket, who was dressed in a simple white kurta but walked with the authority of a prince.

They didn't approach Fauji Baba immediately. He was seated on a decorated stage, surrounded by chants and incense, his hands constantly folded in blessing as a long line of people took turns bowing before him.

Only after the last devotee had moved aside, Aniket step forward and whisper something in his ear.

Fauji Baba turned toward them, his face lighting up the way a mountain glows at dawn.

"Rajendra," he said, rising slightly, his eyes kind.

Rajendra bowed deeply, touching the old man's feet.

"Happy birthday, Gurudev."

Then he stepped aside, and Radha stepped forward with humility and poise.

She bowed. "Many happy returns, Baba."

Fauji Baba looked at her with quiet interest, then at Rajendra. "So this is the Radha I've heard so much about."

Rajendra smiled faintly. "Yes, Gurudev. The one who helped me hold on to light."

Fauji Baba placed a hand on her head and another on Rajendra's shoulder. "God bless you both."

Then his gaze rested on Rajendra again. "I've heard you're doing well in Bhopal. The land has responded. The people are coming."

"I'm only doing what you asked of me," Rajendra replied.

"And next year," Fauji Baba said with a twinkle in his eye, "we will have our grandest ashram yet… right in the land of the lions."

Rajendra nodded. "As you wish, Gurudev."

After the formalities, they stepped off the stage and into the shaded walkways of the ashram. The buzz of celebration continued outside, but Radha's steps had slowed.

Aniket noticed.

"Are you feeling alright?" he asked.

"A little light-headed," she replied.

"You should rest," Aniket said. "I've my room in the inner courtyard. It's peaceful. You can stay there for a while."

Radha nodded, grateful.

Inside Aniket's quarters, the air was cool, the curtains drawn. A soft bed awaited her, along with a jug of lemon water and a plate of fruits.

She sat down but didn't lie back. Something on the wall had caught her eye.

A photograph.

Framed neatly, hung beside a bookshelf.

It showed a man and a woman—smiling, graceful, maybe in their thirties—standing behind a young boy who looked unmistakably like Aniket. It was a classic family portrait. But what caught Radha's attention wasn't the family.

It was the man in the background.

Just barely visible. Blurred slightly by distance.

But smiling. Watching.

She stared at him for a full minute.

Who are you?

She pulled out her phone and took a photo of the photograph. Then she sat, enlarged the image, and studied it again. Something stirred deep in her mind—a vague recognition, like hearing a tune you can't place.

She was still examining it when the door opened.

Rajendra entered with Aniket.

"You look better," Rajendra said.

"I am. Just needed to sit," she replied.

Aniket stepped forward. "Your room is ready now. It's just across the courtyard. You'll rest better there."

Radha got up, but before leaving, she asked, "That photo on the wall… It's your family?"

Aniket nodded casually. "Yes. My parents. And me."

She smiled faintly and walked out.

The next day, when the celebrations had eased and the ashram fell into its usual rhythm, Rajendra and Radha took time for themselves.

They visited the flower temple near Hanuman Mandir, where she once sold garlands, and he came looking for excuses to see her.

They stood at the same peepal tree, where they had shared foods from banana leaves, where their laughter once echoed between the footsteps of devotees.

They didn't talk much. But their silences spoke.

By evening, it was time to leave. As the plane took off from Delhi, Radha looked out the window, eyes brimming.

"Goodbye," she whispered, not to the city... but to something younger inside her.

Back in Bhopal, Rajendra went straight to Panchgarahi Temple for the evening aarti. Radha returned home, hugged her mother, and ate dinner quietly.

But sleep didn't come.

Her mind kept circling the photograph.

She sat on her bed, pulled out her phone, and opened the picture again. The man in the background... where had she seen him?

She opened her sketch pad. Pencil in hand, she began to draw.

First, she sketched what she saw.

Then, instinctively, she changed the hairstyle. Then the beard. Then, age the face by a few years. Then added a pair of spectacles.

One sketch after another. One version of that same face—morphed, matured, rearranged.

An hour passed. Then two.

And then—

She stopped.

Her breath caught.

Her eyes went wide.

The last image on the paper stared back at her—unmistakable now.

She dropped the pencil. The sketch fluttered to the floor.

It was the face of *someone very much alive.*

Radha stared in horror and disbelief.

"It can't be…"

Her voice trembled.

She looked at the paper again. And then whispered in the silence of the room:

"Why is *he* in Aniket's family photo?"

✦✦✦

CHAPTER 25

THE BAIT IN THE BANYAN SHADOWS

The river Narmada flowed like liquid silver beneath the early morning mist. Birds called to one another across the trees, and the air held that rare, divine stillness known only to sacred places.

Aniket had arrived in Bhopal.

Rajendra and Aniket walked along the riverbank, the breeze gently shifting the ends of their robes. Rajendra glanced sideways at the man who had once pulled him from the abyss and now shaped destinies like a sculptor with fire-hardened hands.

Aniket's voice was calm, but charged with intent.
"It's time, Rajendra. We write the final chapter of the Diwan family."

Rajendra stopped for a moment, letting the wind touch his face.
"What are we supposed to do next?"

Aniket didn't turn. He kept walking.
"I'll be conducting a few final surveys… confirming something. But your task begins today. Talk to Dilip. Convince him to do a *Maha Puja* on Poornima night—just you and him. Alone."

Rajendra blinked. "He's not a very spiritual man. Why would he agree?"

Aniket finally turned, eyes steady.
"Because his pride is bruised. His father handed the steel project to Chetan. That wound is still bleeding. He'll do anything to regain control. You must frame this puja as an ancient ritual—one that spiritually reverses betrayal and defeats enemies. Tell him it will help him reclaim his power."

Rajendra nodded slowly, doubt still lingering.
"He might resist…"

Aniket smiled faintly.
"Then push harder. Tell him the ritual requires secrecy. A place untouched by energy—near a *Banyan* tree and a natural water body. He'll likely suggest the old family farmhouse himself. And when he does—act surprised, but agree."

Also, then release the secret of his mother and Chetan. Tell him his mother is also plotting against him. Puja is required to grant him energy to confront his own mother. He will be broken to the core, but support him.

"And Chetan?"

"I'll deal with him," Aniket said coolly. "I'll call him as a *sevak*—someone from the temple who resents your rise. I'll tell him your plan. That you and Dilip are conspiring against him. I'll inflame his thirst for revenge. Also, will tell Dilip now knows your truth that you are the son of Chandraprabha."

Rajendra frowned. "You think he'll fall for that?"

"I know how to press his buttons. I'll encourage him to come in disguise. I'll even suggest he drown Dilip in the pond during the ritual so Mr Diwan doesn't get to know his secret. And before he acts—I'll record enough of his words to make it sound like he planned Dilip's murder."

Rajendra's eyes narrowed. "And Mr. Diwan?"

Aniket's voice dropped to a whisper.
"Once Chetan and Dilip are at the farmhouse and unreachable by phone, I'll send the manipulated video to Mr. Diwan—make it look like Chetan's about to murder his son. I'll urge him to come immediately… alone."

Rajendra stared. "What about Chandraprabha?"

Aniket's eyes glinted.
"Radha will handle her. She'll tell her she overheard Mr. Diwan plotting to have Chetan killed at the farmhouse. The maternal instinct will drag her there like a storm."

Rajendra took a deep breath. "So you want all of them—Chetan, Dilip, Mr. Diwan, and Chandraprabha—to arrive at the same place… each convinced someone they love is about to be destroyed."

Aniket nodded. "That's exactly what I want. Let their lies, secrets, and betrayals combust in one night under that ancient tree. And we… will simply watch."

The mansion buzzed with its usual rituals of power and silence. After lunch, Radha cleaned the final dish and slipped into her usual routine—heading quietly to the dog enclosures at the back, where Ramlal, Sahil's father, spent his days in chains of grief and guilt.

But today, the cell was empty.

"Where is Ramlal Kaka?" she asked the guard on duty.

"Not well," the man replied. "Hasn't come in for two days. Might come tomorrow."

"Do you know where he lives?"

The man hesitated, then pointed. “Behind that big red house—near the old neem tree. He’s got a small quarter there. But don’t go after sunset, beti. Not safe.”

Radha thanked him, mind already planning a visit. But before she could move, a voice rang out from inside the kitchen:

“Radha!” Chandraprabha called.

She returned swiftly, hands wiped, voice steady.

“I want dinner started early. Make Chetan’s Favorites tonight. I want the kitchen perfect,” Chandraprabha ordered without turning.

Radha nodded.
I’ll go tomorrow, she thought.
But something in her gut twisted—an intuition she couldn’t explain.

That night, after the temple lamps had dimmed and the city turned into a hush of rustling trees and distant engines, Rajendra and Aniket sat behind the temple.

“The farmhouse is perfect,” Aniket said, spreading out an old sketch of the place. “Few bedrooms, a huge banyan tree, and a deep pond surrounded by wild grass. There’s an old caretaker. That’s it. No mobile network. No electricity. Just silence and secrets.”

Rajendra studied the map. "You want me to suggest a location with a pond and a Banyan tree.

Let Dilip name the farmhouse himself."

Aniket nodded. "Exactly. But remind him not to tell anyone. Frame it as a *tantric discipline.* Let the secrecy make him believe more."

"And Chetan?"

"I'll provoke him through the temple phone line. I'll tell him about your puja with Dilip is a cover for something darker. He'll come in rage… and greed. I'll offer to help sedate both of you. Then it will be his game."

"And Mr. Diwan?"

Aniket smiled coldly.

"He'll believe what I show him. When he sees the video, hears that Dilip's life is in danger, he'll drive straight toward blood."

Rajendra closed his eyes for a moment.

"What if something goes wrong?"

Aniket stood, his voice steady like a monk's prayer. "Let fate take over. When truth has rotted for too long, destiny writes justice with fire."

Later that night, Rajendra stood on the ashram terrace and dialed a familiar number. The wind was picking up, the clouds thickening like omens.

Radha answered on the second ring.

"Radha," he said softly. "We need to talk."

And under the gaze of a moonless sky, he told her everything.

✦✦✦

CHAPTER 26

THREADS PULLING TIGHT

The morning sun had barely brushed the rooftops when Radha arrived at the Diwan mansion. She moved briskly, her mind racing with the day's urgent agenda.

She had three tasks:

1. Update Aniket and Rajendra about any unusual movements in the Diwan household.
2. Visit Sahil's father, Ramlal, who had stopped coming to the dog kennels.
3. Take Chandraprabha Devi to the old farmhouse.

The kitchen buzzed with morning activity. Radha worked faster than usual, grinding spices, tempering oil, and overseeing the staff with quiet efficiency. But her thoughts kept circling the strange calm inside the Diwan mansion.

Everything looked... normal. Too normal.

Chetan and Dilip, both hiding their plans?

The idea still felt surreal.

At breakfast, Dilip came to the table casually dressed, a hint of cologne and forced ease about him.

"Maa, I'm going to a friend's party today. Might stay the night there," he said, chewing slowly.

Chandraprabha looked up from her tea, smiling. "Good idea, Dilip. You're always drowning in work. Just don't skip meals or drink too much."

A few minutes later, Chetan announced, "I'm off too—need to visit the factory site and handle a few things. I'll be back late, maybe after midnight."

Chandraprabha raised an eyebrow, surprised by both sons leaving at same time. She didn't question it—but something in her face said she noticed.

Soon after, Mr. Diwan himself left, dressed in white linen and crisp confidence. Politics had awakened something in him. With Mahan Baba's recent transfer to Delhi as a central minister, Diwan Singh was now being considered as a serious candidate for Bhopal's upcoming assembly seat.

"I have a meeting with party workers," he told Chandraprabha before heading out. "Will try to be back for lunch."

Chandraprabha nodded and checked her salon appointment on her phone.

By mid-morning, Radha had served breakfast, finished prepping lunch, and wrapped her dupatta to head out. She had no time to lose.

Following the directions given by the staff, Radha made her way to the back alley behind the red bungalow. She spotted the small hut—dilapidated and lonely, the door half-closed.

But no Ramlal.

A neighbor sweeping her front yard looked up and said, "You looking for the old man? He was very weak last night. Some of us took him to the general hospital."

Radha thanked her and rushed off again, praying he was still well enough to speak.

At the hospital, she checked at the reception. A nurse, kind but harried, told her to wait for thirty minutes. "He's getting an IV drip—very dehydrated, very frail. You can go in after that."

Radha sat in the waiting area, tapping her phone nervously. She quickly called Rajendra.

He picked up after two rings.

"I'm with Dilip," he said in a hushed voice. "We're about to leave for the farmhouse. Once we're there, there's no mobile network. I'm sharing the address."

"Okay," Radha whispered, scribbling the location down. "Be careful."

Thirty minutes passed.

Radha was ushered into the hospital ward. Ramlal lay on a rusted iron bed, his body thin and shriveled, his eyes half-sunken. But he recognized her immediately and smiled weakly.

"You came…"

"I brought you some food. You haven't been to the estate. I got worried."

He nodded. "My bones are tired now. The world I knew has already left."

As he ate slowly, she pulled out the picture she had taken in Aniket's room.
She pointed at the man in the background.

"Baba… is this you?"

He squinted, adjusted the angle of the picture in the light. Then, slowly, his eyes widened.

"Yes... that was me. That photo's nearly 25 years old. How did you get this?"

Radha tried to sound casual. "It was hanging on a wall… I was curious. Who are the others in the picture?"

"That's Ramesh—the man in the center. He was a driver for Mr. Diwan. His wife and their little boy... Anku."

Radha felt her chest tighten. "Anku?"

"Yes. Short for Aniket."

The words struck like thunder.

She took a step back, voice dry. "What happened to them?"

Ramlal sighed deeply. "It's a long and painful story. Get me some water…"

After a long sip, he began.

He continued narrating the story. After finishing, he said we never saw Anku after that.

"Some say they all were killed. Others say only the parents were. The boy survived... taken in by a sadhu from the hills. No one knew what happened after."

Radha's breath caught.

The orphan. The sadhu. The boy is named Anku.

Her hands trembled.

"Thank you, Baba," she said quickly. "You've helped more than you know."

She stood, her mind racing. She needed to tell Rajendra—immediately. But when she dialed… the phone was already out of reach.

Just as she turned to rush out, a car honked sharply near the hospital gates.

She looked up.

A black SUV stopped, and from the rear seat, a familiar voice called: "Radha! What are you doing here?"

It was Chandraprabha coming back from the parlor.

Radha froze.

"Come quickly. Mr. Diwan is coming with friends for lunch. We need to start preparation."

Radha hesitated. "But—"

"No time. Get in. Now."

Reluctantly, Radha slid into the seat. The doors locked. The car sped off, rolling toward the Diwan mansion.

And somewhere on a dusty road 20 kilometers outside Bhopal, a car carrying Rajendra and Dilip rolled toward an old, crumbling farmhouse—its pond still, its banyan tree ancient, and its soil hungry for secrets.

✦✦✦

CHAPTER 27

UNDER THE BANYAN, TRUTH AWAKENS

At the old farmhouse, Rajendra moved purposefully, his dhoti tied tight, sweat glistening on his forehead as he arranged the items for the Maha Puja. He laid out brass utensils, sandalwood, ghee lamps, incense, sacred ash, and vermilion near the massive *Banyan* tree. The ground had been cleared. The banyan's roots swayed gently above the sacred soil, casting long shadows across the dying afternoon light.

The silence was eerie.

Inside the house, Dilip wandered curiously, taking in the crumbling ceilings, the fading paint, and old family portraits hanging like ghostly relics. The guard stood nearby, offering polite answers.

"How are things going on here?" Dilip asked casually.

"Going good, saab," the watchman replied. "No one comes anymore. We just keep it from falling apart."

"You need to clean it properly. Look at these cobwebs. Diwali's coming."

"We'll get everything done by this Diwali," the watchman promised.

Dilip chuckled. "How's Heera and Moti? Haven't seen them in years."

The guard's face lit up with a hint of nostalgia and fear.
"They're still alive, saab. Older now—but dangerous as ever. A man comes daily with raw chicken to feed them. We've built a wall around the pond now, so they don't escape."

Then he added nervously, "But sometimes, at night… they make such a splash I feel like they'll leap out and eat me whole!"

Heera and Moti. The Diwan family's most bizarre pets—two crocodiles, once the pride of Diwan Singh, now forgotten in the shadowed pond behind the farmhouse.

Back at the mansion, lunch had been served and devoured with political laughter. Mr. Diwan, pleased with the nod from his party, leaned back in his chair, pride radiating from every wrinkle.

"My ticket for MP is confirmed," he told Chandraprabha, sipping his post-lunch tea. "After that, I'll get a bigger plot… build a mega steel plant for Dilip."

He yawned, stretched, and went to his room to nap before the evening celebration.

But peace was short-lived.

The shrill ring of his phone shattered his rest.

"Hello?" he barked.

A slow, calm voice answered. "Mr. Diwan, listen carefully. Your son… is in danger. Chetan is going to kill Dilip at the farmhouse."

Diwan sat upright. "Who the hell are you? Do you know who you're talking to? One call and the police commissioner will hunt you down like a dog!"

"I'm not your enemy. I'm sending you proof. Check your phone. I'll call back in five minutes."

The call ended abruptly.

A moment later, his phone buzzed. A video arrived.

It showed Chetan—his voice tense, angry—discussing a plan to sedate Rajendra and Dilip during the puja… then push them into the pond. Crocodiles. Blood. Revenge.

Diwan's face turned pale.

He tried calling Dilip—no signal. Chetan—also unreachable.

The phone rang again.

"You saw the video?" the voice asked.

Diwan was breathless. "Who are you?! What do you want?!"

Fifty lakhs. In cash. Bring it to the farmhouse in one hour. Come alone. Reach before Dilip arrives… or your son will never come back."

Click.

One kilometer away from the farmhouse, Chetan's jeep idled beside the road. Aniket approached calmly, pocketing the phone just after the call.

"You took your time," Chetan snapped. "Fifteen minutes, I've been waiting for your pee break."

Aniket smiled apologetically. "Baba called from Delhi. Important talk. Come, let's go."

They drove toward the farmhouse, the sky darkening, clouds roiling like coiled snakes.

Meanwhile, Diwan Singh grabbed a black duffel bag, stuffed it with cash, and stormed outside.

"Driver! Start the car—NOW!"

Chandraprabha ran after him. "Where are you going? You look pale—what happened?!"

"No time! I'll explain later!"

The car engine roared to life. She chased but couldn't catch. The car vanished.

Heart pounding, Chandraprabha dialed Dilip. Switched off. Then Chetan. Nothing.

Her hands trembled.

Something's wrong.

Radha stepped forward from the courtyard shadows.

Chandraprabha looked at her, distraught. "Radha, do you know who Mr. Diwan was talking to when you took tea for him? Did you hear anything?"

Radha lowered her voice. "Madam… I wasn't sure I should say this. But while I was taking tea to his room, I overheard a call. Someone said Chetan has taken Dilip to the some old farmhouse. He plans to kill him."

Chandraprabha's face went pale. "What?! That's impossible! Chetan would never—"

"I heard it with my own ears," Radha whispered. "Please do something."

Tears pricked her eyes. "God, what is happening to this family…"

She rushed to the garage. "Driver! Take the car out—we're going to the farmhouse. Hurry!"

Radha followed, concerned. "It's not safe at night, Madam. Let me come with you."

Chandraprabha hesitated… then nodded. "Fine. Come."

The car surged forward.

Toward the old farmhouse.

Toward the pond.

Toward the shadows of the Banyan.

✦✦✦

CHAPTER 28

BENEATH THE BANYAN MOON

It was Poornima full moon night.

A full moon watched silently from the heavens, casting silver light across the ancient farmhouse, the whispering fields, and the still, black pond. The *Banyan* tree stood tall and quiet, its shadow stretching like a wound across the earth.

Near its roots, Rajendra Guru sat cross-legged, his hands weaving through the sacred rituals of the *Maha Puja*. The flames flickered in rhythm with his chants. Across from him sat Dilip, back straight, hands folded, eyes closed in reverence—or was it fear?

A copper bowl was passed.

"Take this water," Rajendra said softly.

Dilip took a sip.

Hidden inside a dimly lit room of the farmhouse, Chetan and Aniket Guru watched, breath held, eyes focused. The watchman was gone—scared off by Chetan's earlier threats.

Aniket leaned close to Chetan and whispered, "The sedative is in the water. Dilip will fall asleep soon."

"But what about Rajendra Guru?" Chetan asked.

Aniket's smile was cold. "He always drinks from his own copper bottle between rituals. That, too, is ready."

Moments later, Rajendra reached for his bottle and took a long sip.
The chants slowed. The air thickened. The moon climbed higher.

And then… silence.

Both men collapsed beside the fire.

"Let's move," Aniket said. "Drag them near the pond. Morning will bring headlines: 'Diwan's beloved pets feast on his own blood.'"

Chetan hesitated. "How do you even know about the crocodiles?"

"I grew up nearby," Aniket replied. "Heera and Moti are legends… as is the cruelty of their master."

A short distance away, Mr. Diwan's car screeched to a halt.

He barked at his driver to stay behind and sprinted through the shadows of the farm, breath ragged, the bag of cash slamming against his side.

And there—by the moon-drenched pond—he saw it.

Chetan is dragging an unconscious Dilip toward the edge.

"STOP! CHETAN! WHAT ARE YOU DOING?!" Diwan roared, his voice cutting through the night.

Chetan froze.

In a panic, he tried to shove Dilip into the pond.
A glint of metal.
A gunshot split the air.

Then another.

Chetan fell, blood pooling like a dark flower at his chest.

But it was too late.
Dilip's body had slipped into the pond.

The still water stirred.

Heera. Moti.
The ancient crocodiles, now awakened, rushed toward the splashing body.

Diwan ran, screaming, toward the gate, wrenching it open and diving to pull Dilip out.

But the gods weren't listening tonight.

Heera caught Dilip.
Diwan grabbed him and pulled.
Then Moti struck.

A shriek. A struggle. And then—

Silence.

Only ripples remained.

The crocodiles had taken their final command.
Two of the Diwan men. Gone.

From a distance, Chandraprabha Devi's car arrived, headlights casting wide arcs across the broken farmhouse. She had heard the gunshots. Fear clawed at her chest.

Radha sat beside her, holding her hand.

They arrived just in time to hear the splashing, to see Diwan's form disappear into the pond, and to hear the ghastly wet snaps of jaws under the full moon.

Chandraprabha ran to the edge of the pond, her screams tearing through the night.

"My sons! My husband!"

She collapsed to her knees.

From the shadows, Rajendra also got up from his pretended sedation. He turned toward Aniket, who stood a few feet away—smiling.

Radha ran to Rajendra, grabbing his hand.
"Raju... I need to tell you something."

Her words came in waves—raw, broken, unstoppable.

"Aniket Guru is Anku—his real name. Son of Ramesh, the old driver who once worked for Mr. Diwan. Twenty-five years ago, they lived here. On Diwan's 40th birthday, an imported dog was gifted to him. One day, the dog attacked Anku. His parents rushed to protect him, pushed the dog away, and by mistake, it fell into the pond. The crocodiles devoured it."

Rajendra's face stiffened.

Radha continued, eyes wide with the horror she'd heard.

"Diwan was angry to his core hearing that. That dog was beloved to him. The next day... Diwan called Anku and his parents to the pond. He pointed a gun at ten-year-old Anku. Told the parents to jump in or he'd shoot the boy. They pleaded. They begged. Nothing touched him. To save their son, they took a promise from Mr

Diwan not to harm their son, they leapt in… and the crocodiles…"

Her voice cracked.

"Anku watched them die. Helpless. Screaming."

Aniket stepped forward, clapping slowly.

"Well said, Radha. My past, laid bare. I was the shadow. The whisper. The boy who survived. You now know *why* I returned."

Rajendra's voice was quiet. "So this was all… revenge?"

Aniket's face darkened. "Justice. The system protects the Diwans of this world. But fate—fate remembers."

He stepped toward them, eyes shining with both madness and calm.

"Oh, and Rajni? The daughter of that devil? I brought her to Delhi. Played the part of a kind lawyer, helping runaways. I lured her in… delivered her to the same men Diwan had hired to kill her. He thought he controlled the chessboard. He never saw the pawn become a king."

He turned away, arms raised to the moon.

"Tonight, the bloodline ends. The pond has been fed. The Banyan has witnessed."

Behind them, Chandraprabha was still screaming by the water's edge, as if her cries could rewind time.

Radha leaned into Rajendra's shoulder, voice hollow.

"We were helping him all along. We thought it was our cause. Our war."

Rajendra's eyes were distant.

"No. We were pawns. Revenge wears many faces—some noble, some monstrous."

He turned to look at the full moon.

"Violence doesn't end with justice. It ends when someone chooses not to retaliate. But tonight, that choice was buried with the Diwan name."

Radha whispered, "Was this justice… or just another tragedy?"

Rajendra did not answer.

The Banyan tree swayed gently in the wind. The pond was still. The moon bore witness, as it always had.

And somewhere deep in its roots, old blood soaked quietly into the soil.

Aniket's laughter rose like wild thunder dancing through madness, while Rajendra drifted in a haze of thought, tangled in the riddles of unfolding fate. Beneath the robes, ashes poured forth in silent descent.

**** THE END ****